The Madman of Bergerac

'I love reading Simenon. He makes me think of Chekhov'
– William Faulkner

'A truly wonderful writer . . . marvellously readable – lucid, simple, absolutely in tune with the world he creates'
– Muriel Spark

'Few writers have ever conveyed with such a sure touch, the bleakness of human life'
– A. N. Wilson

'One of the greatest writers of the twentieth century . . . Simenon was unequalled at making us look inside, though the ability was masked by his brilliance at absorbing us obsessively in his stories'
– *Guardian*

'A novelist who entered his fictional world as if he were part of it'
– Peter Ackroyd

'The greatest of all, the most genuine novelist we have had in literature'
– André Gide

'Superb . . . The most addictive of writers . . . A unique teller of tales'
– *Observer*

'The mysteries of the human personality are revealed in all their disconcerting complexity'
– Anita Brookner

'A writer who, more than any other crime novelist, combined a high literary reputation with popular appeal'
– P. D. James

'A supreme writer . . . Unforgettable vividness'
– *Independent*

'Compelling, remorseless, brilliant'
– John Gray

'Extraordinary masterpieces of the twentieth century'
– John Banville

ABOUT THE AUTHOR

Georges Simenon was born on 12 February 1903 in Liège, Belgium, and died in 1989 in Lausanne, Switzerland, where he had lived for the latter part of his life. Between 1931 and 1972 he published seventy-five novels and twenty-eight short stories featuring Inspector Maigret.

Simenon always resisted identifying himself with his famous literary character, but acknowledged that they shared an important characteristic:

> My motto, to the extent that I have one, has been noted often enough, and I've always conformed to it. It's the one I've given to old Maigret, who resembles me in certain points . . . 'understand and judge not'.

Penguin is publishing the entire series of Maigret novels.

GEORGES SIMENON

The Madman of Bergerac

Translated by ROS SCHWARTZ

PENGUIN BOOKS

PENGUIN CLASSICS

Published by the Penguin Group
Penguin Books Ltd, 80 Strand, London WC2R ORL, England
Penguin Group (USA) Inc., 375 Hudson Street, New York, New York 10014, USA
Penguin Group (Canada), 90 Eglinton Avenue East, Suite 700, Toronto, Ontario, Canada M4P 2Y3
(a division of Pearson Penguin Canada Inc.)
Penguin Ireland, 25 St Stephen's Green, Dublin 2, Ireland (a division of Penguin Books Ltd)
Penguin Group (Australia), 707 Collins Street, Melbourne, Victoria 3008, Australia
(a division of Pearson Australia Group Pty Ltd)
Penguin Books India Pvt Ltd, 11 Community Centre, Panchsheel Park, New Delhi – 110 017, India
Penguin Group (NZ), 67 Apollo Drive, Rosedale, Auckland 0632, New Zealand
(a division of Pearson New Zealand Ltd)
Penguin Books (South Africa) (Pty) Ltd, Block D, Rosebank Office Park, 181 Jan Smuts Avenue,
Parktown North, Gauteng 2193, South Africa

Penguin Books Ltd, Registered Offices: 80 Strand, London WC2R ORL, England

www.penguin.com

First published in French as Les trois morts de Bergerac by Fayard 1932
This translation first published in Penguin Books 2015
002

Copyright 1932 by Georges Simenon Limited
Translation copyright © Ros Schwartz, 2015
GEORGES SIMENON ® Simenon.tm
MAIGRET ® Georges Simenon Limited
All rights reserved

The moral rights of the author and translator have been asserted

Set in Dante MT Std 12.5/15 pt
Typeset by Palimpsest Book Production Ltd, Falkirk, Stirlingshire
Printed in Great Britain by Clays Ltd, St Ives plc

ISBN: 978-0-141-39456-5

www.greenpenguin.co.uk

Contents

1. *The Restless Passenger*

It all came about by pure chance! The previous day, Maigret had not known that he was about to go on a journey, even though it was the time of year when he usually began to find Paris oppressive. It was a March spiced up with a fore-taste of spring and a clear, sharp sun that was already warm.

Madame Maigret was away in Alsace for a couple of weeks, staying with her sister, who was having a baby.

On the Wednesday morning, the inspector received a letter from a former colleague who had retired from the Police Judiciaire two years earlier and moved to the Dordogne.

> . . . *And of course, if you happen to be in the area, do come and stay with me for a few days. I have an elderly housekeeper who is only too happy when there are guests to fuss over. And it's the start of the salmon season—*

Maigret's imagination was particularly fired by the letter-head with its drawing of a manor house flanked by two circular towers above the address:

La Ribaudière
near Villefranche-en-Dordogne

At midday, Madame Maigret telephoned from Alsace to say that her sister would probably give birth that night, adding, 'You'd think it was summer . . . The fruit trees are in blossom!'

Chance . . . Pure chance . . . A little later, Maigret was in the chief's office, chatting, when his superior said, 'By the way . . . Did you ever go to Bordeaux to follow up that matter we talked about?'

It was a minor case of no urgency. At some point, Maigret had to go to Bordeaux to trawl through the municipal records.

One idea led to another: Bordeaux . . . the Dordogne.

At that exact moment, a ray of sunlight struck the crystal globe paperweight on the chief's desk.

'That's a thought! I'm not working on anything at the moment.'

Later that afternoon, having purchased a first-class ticket to Villefranche, Maigret boarded the train at the Gare d'Orsay. The guard reminded him to change trains at Libourne.

'Unless you're in the sleeper compartment which gets hitched to the connecting train.'

Maigret thought no more about it, read a few newspapers and made his way to the dining car where he sat until ten o'clock.

When he returned to his compartment, he found the curtains drawn and the light dimmed. An elderly couple had commandeered both seats.

An attendant walked past.

'Is there a free bunk by any chance?'

'Not in first-class . . . but I think there's one in second . . . If you don't mind—'

'Of course not!'

And Maigret lugged his carpet-bag along the corridors. The attendant opened several doors and finally found the compartment in which only the upper bunk was taken.

Here too, the light was dimmed and the curtains drawn.

'Would you like me to switch on the light?'

'No thank you.'

The air was warm and stuffy. There was a faint hissing sound, as if there was a leak in the radiator pipes. Maigret could hear the person in the top bunk tossing and turning and breathing heavily.

The inspector silently removed his shoes, jacket and waistcoat. He stretched out on the lower bunk and felt a slight draught coming from somewhere. He picked up his bowler hat and put it over his face for protection.

Did he fall asleep? He dozed off, in any case. Perhaps for an hour, perhaps two. Perhaps longer. But he remained half conscious.

And, in that semi-conscious state, he was aware of a feeling of discomfort. Was it because of the heat battling with the draught?

Or was it because of the man in the top bunk, who couldn't keep still for a second? He tossed and turned continually, just above Maigret's head. Every movement made a rustling sound.

His breathing was irregular, as if he had a fever.

After a time, Maigret got up, exasperated, went into

the corridor and paced up and down. But there it was too cold.

So it was back into the compartment, and another attempt to sleep, his thoughts and sensations befuddled by drowsiness.

Cut off from the rest of the world, the atmosphere was that of a nightmare.

Had the man above him just raised himself up on his elbows and leaned over to try and get a look at his companion?

Maigret, meanwhile, didn't dare move. The half-bottle of Bordeaux and the two brandies he had drunk in the dining car lay heavy in his stomach.

The night was long. Whenever the train stopped at a station, there was a babble of voices, footsteps in the corridors, doors slamming. It felt as if the train would never get going again.

It sounded as if the man was crying. There were moments when he held his breath. Then suddenly, there'd be a snivel and he would turn over and blow his nose.

Maigret regretted leaving his first-class compartment occupied by the elderly couple.

He dozed off, woke up and drifted off again. Finally, unable to stand it any longer, he coughed to steady his voice and said, 'Monsieur, would you kindly try to keep still!'

He felt embarrassed, because his voice sounded much sterner than he had intended. Supposing the man was ill?

There was no answer. The tossing and turning stopped. The man must have been making a huge effort to avoid making the slightest sound. And it suddenly occurred to Maigret that it might not be a man after all, but a woman! He hadn't seen the person who was wedged between the bunk and the ceiling.

And the heat must be suffocating up there. Now Maigret tried to turn down the radiator, but the control knob was jammed.

It was three o'clock in the morning.

'I really must get some sleep!'

Now he was wide awake. He had become almost as jumpy as his fellow passenger. He listened out.

'Here we go! He's at it again.'

And Maigret forced himself to breathe regularly and count sheep, in the hope of falling asleep.

The man was definitely crying! Probably someone who had been to Paris for a funeral. Or vice versa, a poor soul who worked in Paris and had received bad news from back home – his mother ill, or dead . . . Or maybe his wife . . . Maigret was sorry he'd been harsh with him. You never knew . . . Sometimes they hitched a special hearse wagon to the train.

His thoughts turned to his sister-in-law in Alsace who was about to give birth. Three children in four years!

Maigret slept.

The train halted, then moved off again. It clattered over an iron bridge, making a terrible racket, and Maigret was suddenly wide awake.

Then he froze at the sight of two legs dangling in front of his nose. The man was sitting on his bunk meticulously lacing up his shoes. It was the first thing that the inspector saw of him and, despite the dim light, he noticed that they were patent-leather shoes. His socks, meanwhile, were grey wool and looked hand-knitted.

The man paused and listened. Had he noticed the change in Maigret's breathing pattern?

Maigret started counting sheep again. It was all the more difficult because he was intrigued by the hands tying the shoelaces. They were trembling so badly that it took the man four attempts to tie the bow.

The train shot through a small station without stopping. All that could be seen through the curtain fabric were the lights flashing past.

The man was coming down! This was slowly turning into a nightmare. Why couldn't he descend in an ordinary fashion? Was he afraid of being rebuked again?

His foot groped for the ladder for ages. He almost tumbled from the bunk. Then, keeping his back to the inspector, the man left the compartment, without bothering to close the door, and headed for the end of the corridor.

Had it not been for the open door, Maigret would probably have turned over and tried to go back to sleep. But he had to get up to shut it. He looked up and down the corridor.

He just had the time to throw on his jacket, not bothering with the waistcoat.

For the stranger had opened the carriage door at the far end of the corridor. It was not by chance: he had opened it just as the train was slowing down.

They were passing a forest. There were a few clouds illuminated by an invisible moon.

The brakes squealed. The train had slowed down from eighty kilometres an hour to around thirty, perhaps even less.

The man jumped off and slipped down the embankment, then vanished in the darkness. Maigret barely stopped to think. He leaped. The train was going even slower now, so he wasn't in any danger.

He landed on his side and rolled over three times, coming to rest by a barbed-wire fence.

The train's red light moved off and the clatter of the wheels grew fainter.

Maigret stood up. He hadn't broken any bones. His companion's fall must have been much harder, for he could see him, fifty metres away, still struggling to get to his feet.

This situation was ridiculous. Maigret wondered what instinct had prompted him to jump off the train while his luggage continued on its way to Villefranche-en-Dordogne. He didn't even know where he was!

He could see nothing but woodland – probably a vast forest. Further away the pale ribbon of a road plunged into the trees.

Why was the man not moving? All Maigret could see was a kneeling shadow. Had he realized he was being followed? Was he hurt?

'Hey! You over there!' shouted Maigret fumbling for the gun in his pocket.

He didn't have time to grab it. He saw a flash of red. And he felt something hit his shoulder even before hearing the report.

The whole thing hadn't lasted a tenth of a second and

already the man had sprung up, sprinted through a copse, crossed the main road and vanished into the pitch darkness.

Maigret cursed. Tears sprang to his eyes, not from the pain, but from shock, rage and confusion. It had all happened so fast! And he was in such a sorry mess!

He dropped his gun, bent down to pick it up and winced because his shoulder hurt.

No, it was something else: the sensation that he was bleeding profusely, that with each heartbeat the warm blood was spurting from a severed artery.

He didn't dare run. He didn't dare move. He didn't even pick up his weapon.

His temples were damp, his throat tight. And, as expected, when he touched his shoulder, his hand came into contact with a sticky liquid. He squeezed and felt for the artery with his fingertips to staunch the flow of blood.

In his semi-conscious state, Maigret had the impression that less than a kilometre away, the train had been stationary for a long, long time while he listened out, acutely anxious.

What could it matter to him if the train had stopped? His response was automatic. The absence of the wheels' rumbling left a void which terrified him.

At last! The noise started up again in the distance. He glimpsed something red moving in the sky, behind the trees.

Then nothing.

Maigret stood utterly alone, clutching his shoulder with his right hand. It was his left shoulder that had been hit.

He tried to move his left arm and managed to raise it slightly, but it flopped back again, too heavy.

The woods were completely silent, suggesting that the man had not fled but was hiding in the undergrowth. If Maigret tried to reach the main road, might he not shoot again to finish him off?

'Idiot! Idiot! Idiot!' muttered Maigret, who felt utterly wretched.

Why had he felt the urge to jump off the train? At dawn his friend Leduc would be waiting for him at Villefranche station and his housekeeper would have cooked a salmon.

Maigret walked listlessly. He was forced to stop after three metres. He set off again, stopped once more.

Only the pale road stood out in the blackness, white and dusty like at the height of summer. Maigret was still bleeding, but not so profusely. His hand was stemming the flow and was covered in blood.

You would never have guessed that he had been wounded three times before. He was as scared as if on an operating table. He would prefer acute pain to this slow ebbing of blood.

It would be stupid to die here, tonight, all alone. Without even knowing where he was! While his luggage continued on its way without him!

'Too bad if the man shoots!' He walked as fast as he could, lurching forwards, feeling giddy. There was a signpost. But only the right hand side was lit up by a halo of moonlight: *3.5 km*.

What was at 3.5 km? Which town? Which village?

A cow mooed from that direction where the sky was a

little paler. That was probably the east. Dawn was about to break!

The stranger must have moved on. Or he had decided against trying to finish off the wounded inspector. Maigret calculated that he still had the strength to keep going for three or four minutes, and tried to make the most of it. He walked like a soldier, with regular steps, counting to stop himself from thinking.

The mooing cow must belong to a farm. Farmers rise early . . . Therefore—

The blood was seeping down his left side, beneath his shirt, beneath his trouser belt.

Was that a light he could see? Was he delirious already?

'If I lose more than a litre of blood—' he thought.

It was a light. But there was a ploughed field to cross and that was more difficult. His feet sank into the mud. He brushed past an abandoned tractor.

'Hello! . . . Someone! . . . Help! Quick!'

That desperate *quick* escaped him as he leaned against the tractor for support. He slid down and sat on the ground. He heard a door opening and made out a lantern swinging on the end of an arm.

'Quick!'

Hopefully the man who was coming over, getting closer, would be sharp-witted enough to staunch the bleeding! Meanwhile Maigret's hand lost its grip and fell limply to his side.

'One . . . two . . . one . . . two . . .'

The blood spurted out with every count.

★

Confused images, with blanks in between. All of them tinged with that note of panic that is the stuff of dreams.

A rhythm . . . The clip-clop of hooves . . . Straw under his head and trees filing past on his right.

That much, Maigret understood. He was lying in a cart. It was light. They were plodding slowly along a road lined with plane trees.

He opened his eyes without moving. Eventually a man entered his field of vision. He was sauntering along the road swinging a whip.

A nightmare? Maigret hadn't seen the face of the man from the train. All he knew of him was a vague form, patent-leather shoes and grey woollen socks.

So why did he think that the man leading the cart was the man from the train?

He saw a deeply lined face, with a bushy grey moustache and heavy eyebrows . . . and light-coloured eyes looking straight ahead, taking no notice of the wounded man.

Where were they? Where were they going?

Maigret's hand moved and he felt a strange wad around his chest, like a thick dressing.

Then his thoughts became muddled just as a ray of sunshine bored through his eyes into his brain.

Later there were houses, white façades . . . A wide street, bathed in light. Noise behind the cart, the noise of a crowd on the move . . . and voices . . . but he couldn't make out the words. The bumping made his wound hurt.

No more jolts . . . Just a swaying movement now, a rolling that he had never experienced before.

He was on a stretcher. In front of him was a man in a

white coat. A big gate clanged shut behind them and on the other side was a milling crowd. There was a sound of running footsteps.

'Take him to the operating theatre right away.'

He didn't move his head. He didn't think. But he looked.

They were crossing lawns dotted with small, pristine buildings. Men in grey uniforms sat on benches. Some had their heads or legs bandaged. Nurses were bustling about.

And in his sluggish mind, he tried, without success, to formulate the word 'hospital'.

Where was the farmer who looked like the man on the train? Ouch! They were going up some stairs. That hurt.

Maigret came to again to see a man washing his hands and looking at him gravely.

His heart skipped a beat. The man had a goatee, and busy eyebrows!

Did he look like the farmer? In any case, he looked like the man from the train!

Maigret couldn't speak. He opened his mouth. The man with the goatee said calmly, 'Put him in number three. It's best for him to be in isolation because of the police.'

Because of the police? What did he mean?

People in white transported him through the grounds again. The sunshine was brighter than any sunshine Maigret had ever seen – a sun so strong, so powerful, it seemed to reach the farthest recesses!

They were putting him in a bed. The walls were white. It was almost as hot as in the train. A voice was saying, 'It's the inspector who's asking when he'll be able to—'

The inspector – wasn't he the inspector? He hadn't asked

anything! This was ridiculous! Especially this business with the farmer who looked like the doctor and the man on the train!

But did the man on the train have a grey goatee? A moustache? Bushy eyebrows?

'Unclench his teeth . . . Good . . . Enough.'

The doctor was pouring something into his mouth.

To finish him off by poisoning him, of course!

When Maigret came round, towards evening, the nurse who was watching over him went out into the corridor where five men were waiting: the investigating magistrate from Bergerac, the prosecutor, the police inspector, a court clerk and the forensic pathologist.

'You may go in, but the doctor advises you not to tire him. He has such a strange look that I wouldn't be surprised if he's mad!'

And the five men exchanged knowing glances.

2. Five Disappointed Men

The nurse had left the room, smiling and glancing over her shoulder at Maigret.

A glance that meant, 'I'll leave you to it!'

The ensuing scene was like something from a melodrama played by ham actors. The five gentlemen took over the room, all of them smiling in a different way, all equally menacing. As if this weren't real, as if they were deliberately playing a good old joke on Maigret!

'After you, prosecutor, sir.'

A short man sporting a crew cut and a moustache with a fearsome gaze, who must have worked hard to create a look that befitted his profession. And an affectation of frostiness, of meanness!

He merely walked past Maigret's bed, gave him a fleeting look then went to stand in front of the wall, hat in hand, as if at a ceremony.

And the investigating magistrate also paraded past, sneering at the injured Maigret, and took his place beside his chief.

Then the clerk . . . The three of them stood lined up against the wall like three conspirators! And now the pathologist had joined them!

The only person left was the podgy police inspector with bulging eyes, who was to play the part of executioner.

A wink at the others. Then his hand came down slowly on Maigret's shoulder.

'Caught, eh!'

At any other time, Maigret might have found this highly amusing, but he did not even smile. He creased his forehead with concern.

Concern for his own person! It felt to him as if the fine line between reality and dream, which was always fuzzy, was being erased with each passing moment.

And now they were acting out this farcical investigation! The grotesque police inspector had a devious look.

'I must say I'm glad to clap eyes on you at last!'

The four others standing against the wall looked on without batting an eyelid.

Maigret surprised himself by letting out a long sigh and taking his right hand out from beneath the sheet.

'Where were you after last night? Another woman, or a girl?' interrogated the inspector. Only then did Maigret realize how much explaining he would have to do to remedy the situation, and was aghast. He was exhausted. He was sleepy. His entire body ached.

'Too much—' he stammered mechanically, giving a limp wave.

The others did not understand. He repeated in a whisper, 'Too much . . . Tomorrow—'

And he closed his eyes. Soon the prosecutor, the magistrate, the pathologist, the inspector and the clerk all merged into one person who resembled the surgeon, the farmer and the man from the train.

★

The following morning, he was sitting up in bed, or rather he was propped up on two pillows, watching the nurse bustling about in the sunshine as she tidied the room.

She was a lovely girl, tall and strong, an aggressive blonde, who kept looking at the wounded man in a way that was both provocative and apprehensive.

'Tell me . . . Five gentlemen came yesterday, is that right?'

She snorted disdainfully, 'That won't wash with me!'

'Very well . . . So tell me what they were doing here.'

'I'm forbidden to speak to you and you'd better know that I will repeat anything you tell me!'

Bizarrely, Maigret was half enjoying his predicament. It was like waking in the morning in the middle of a dream that you are determined to finish before being fully awake.

The sun shone as brightly as in a fairy tale. Outside, soldiers were riding past on horseback, and when they turned the street corner, there was a victorious fanfare of trumpets.

Just then, the nurse walked past the bed and Maigret, wanting to attract her attention to ask more questions, tweaked the hem of her dress between two fingers.

She wheeled round, let out a terrified shriek and fled.

Things did not improve until a little before midday. The surgeon was removing Maigret's dressing when the police inspector arrived. He wore a brand new straw hat and a royal-blue necktie.

'You didn't even have the curiosity to open my wallet?' Maigret asked him amiably.

'You know very well that you have no wallet!'

'All right, I can explain everything. Telephone the Police Judiciaire. They'll inform you that I am Detective Chief Inspector Maigret. If you want to speed things up, contact my colleague Leduc, who has a country house in Ville-franche. But first of all, please tell me where I am!'

The local inspector stood his ground. He kept giving knowing smiles and even nudging the surgeon discreetly with his elbow. Until the arrival of Leduc, who rolled up in an old Ford, they all remained on their guard.

Eventually, they had to agree that Maigret was indeed Maigret and not *the madman of Bergerac*!

Leduc had the florid pink complexion of a man of independent means. Since his retirement from the Police Judiciaire, he affected to smoke nothing but a meerschaum pipe whose cherrywood stem poked out of his pocket.

'Here's the story in a nutshell. I'm not from Bergerac, but I drive in every Saturday for the market and I take the opportunity to enjoy a good dinner at the Hôtel d'Angleterre . . . Well, about a month ago, a dead woman was found on the main road . . . Strangled, to be exact . . . but not just strangled! . . . Once she was dead, the murderer had sadistically stabbed her in the heart with a giant needle.'

'Who was the woman?'

'Léontine Moreau, from the Moulin-Neuf farm. Nothing had been stolen from her.'

'And had she been—?'

'No, she hadn't been molested, even though she was a beautiful woman of around thirty. The murder took place at nightfall, when she was on her way home from her sister-in-law's . . . That was the first! . . . The second—'

'There are two?'

'Two and a half . . . The other is a girl of sixteen, the stationmaster's daughter, who had gone for a bicycle ride . . . She was found in the same state.'

'At night?'

'The following morning. But the murder was committed at night. And the third is a chambermaid at the hotel. She had been to visit her brother, a roadmender who works five or six kilometres away. She was on foot. Suddenly, someone grabbed her from behind and pulled her over . . . but she's strong . . . She managed to bite the man's wrist . . . He swore and ran away. She only caught a vague glimpse of his back, as he ran through the undergrowth.'

'Is that all?'

'That's all! People are convinced that it's a madman who's hiding in the local woods. No one will admit the possibility that it could be someone from the town. When the farmer told us that he'd found you on the road, we all thought you were the murderer and that you'd been injured attempting to kill another woman.'

Leduc was solemn. He did not appear to see the funny side of this mix-up.

'What's more,' he added, 'there are people who won't budge on this.'

'Who is investigating the murders?'

'The prosecutor's office and the local police.'

'Let me sleep, will you?'

All Maigret wanted was to sleep, probably because he

was so weak. He could only manage to stay half-awake, keeping his eyes closed, preferably with the sun on his face, shining on his eyelids.

Now, he had new characters to think about, to bring to life mentally, the way a boy makes brightly coloured toy soldiers march up and down.

The thirty-year-old farm woman . . . The stationmaster's daughter . . . The hotel chambermaid.

He remembered the woods with their tall trees and the pale road, and he imagined the attack, the victim rolling in the dust, the man brandishing the long needle.

It was incredible! Especially thinking about it in this hospital room soothed by the peaceful noises from the street below. Someone spent at least ten minutes trying to crank-start their car, right beneath Maigret's window. The surgeon arrived in a fast, sleek car which he drove himself.

It was eight o'clock in the evening and the lamps were lit when he leaned over Maigret's bed.

'Is it serious, doctor?'

'The main thing is that this is going to take time. Two weeks of bed rest.'

'Couldn't I go and stay at a hotel?'

'Aren't you comfortable here? Of course, if you have someone to nurse you—'

'Tell me, in confidence, what do you think about this Bergerac madman?'

The doctor said nothing for a while. Maigret pressed him.

'Do you think, like everyone else, that he's some lunatic who lives in the woods?'

'No!'

Of course not! Maigret had had the time to reflect and to recall similar cases he had investigated or heard about.

'A man who, in everyday life, probably behaves just like you or me, isn't that so?'

'It is possible!'

'In other words, there's a strong chance that he lives in Bergerac and that he practises some profession.'

The surgeon shot him a quizzical look, faltered and looked flustered.

'Do you have any ideas?' went on Maigret without taking his eyes off him.

'I've had several, one after the other . . . I consider them . . . I reject them indignantly . . . I reconsider them . . . Looked at in a particular light, every person could potentially become deranged.'

Maigret laughed.

'And you work your way through the entire town! From the mayor and even the prosecutor down to the first person to walk past. Not forgetting your colleagues, the hospital porter—'

The surgeon wasn't laughing.

'Just a moment . . . Hold still,' he said, probing the wound with a fine blade. 'It's much worse than you think—'

'What's the population of Bergerac?'

'Around 16,000. Everything points to him coming from a higher social class . . . and even—'

'The needle, of course!' muttered Maigret, wincing because the surgeon was hurting him.

'What do you mean?'

'That the needle accurately piercing the heart in both cases already proves he has a knowledge of anatomy.'

There was silence. The surgeon had a worried frown. He re-did the dressing around Maigret's shoulder and chest, and straightened up with a sigh.

'You were saying you would rather be in a hotel room?'

'Yes, I'd get my wife to come.'

'Do you want to investigate this case?'

'You bet I do!'

Rain would have ruined everything. But there hadn't been a drop for at least two weeks.

Maigret was ensconced in the best room of the Hôtel d'Angleterre, on the first floor. His bed had been moved over to the window so he could enjoy the sight of the main square where he could watch the shade move slowly across from one row of houses to the one on the opposite side.

Unsurprised and unruffled, Madame Maigret took the situation in her stride, as she did everything. She had only been in the room for an hour and already it had become her room, full of her creature comforts, her personal touch.

She must have been the same in Alsace, two days earlier, at her sister's bedside during the birth.

'A big baby girl! You should see her! She weighs nearly five kilos.'

She quizzed the surgeon, 'What can he eat, doctor? Some nice chicken soup? There's one thing you should ban, and that's his pipe! And beer! In an hour's time, he'll be asking me for one.'

It was an immense room with two beds and a 200-year-old fireplace in which a cheap radiator had been installed. The walls were covered in startling red-and-green wallpaper. Blood red! Bright green! Long stripes that sang in the sunshine. And the varnished cheap pine hotel furniture wobbled on its spindly legs!

'What I want to know is why you jumped off the train after that man. Supposing you'd fallen on to the track. The thought of it! I'm going to make you some lemon curd. I hope they'll let me use the kitchen.'

Moments of reverie were rarer now. Even when he closed his eyes in a ray of sunshine, Maigret was more or less clear-headed.

But he continued to think about characters created or pieced together by his imagination.

The first victim . . . The farm woman . . . Married? Children?

Married to a farmer's son, but she didn't get on with her mother-in-law who accused her of being coquettish and wearing silk petticoats to milk the cows.

Then, patiently, lovingly, the way a painter fills in a canvas, Maigret built up a portrait of the farm woman, whom he imagined as delectable, plump and well groomed, browsing through catalogues from Paris and bringing modern ideas into her in-laws' house.

She had been on her way back from town. He could picture the road clearly. The roads around here must all be alike, lined with tall trees casting a shadow on either side . . . and the white, chalky soil, shimmering in the faintest ray of sunshine.

Then the girl on her bicycle.

Did she have a suitor?

There had been no mention of one! Every year, she would go and spend two weeks' holiday at an aunt's in Paris.

The bed was damp. The surgeon came twice a day. After lunch, Leduc arrived in his Ford and manoeuvred clumsily beneath the window in order to park tidily.

On the third morning, he too wore a straw hat, just like the police inspector.

The prosecutor paid a visit. He mistook Madame Maigret for the maid and handed her his walking stick and bowler hat.

'I hope you'll forgive the misunderstanding . . . but the fact that you had no identification on you—'

'Yes! My wallet disappeared. But please sit down, dear monsieur.'

There was still something aggressive about the prosecutor. He couldn't help it. It was because of his little bulbous nose and his stiff, bristly moustache.

'This appalling case is destroying the calm of this beautiful region. One would understand if it had happened in Paris, where vice is endemic . . . but here!'

Damn it! He too had bushy eyebrows! Like the farmer! Like the doctor! Grey eyebrows which Maigret automatically associated with the man from the train!

And a walking stick with a carved ivory knob.

'All the same, I hope you will make a speedy recovery and that you won't have too bad a memory of our area!'

It was merely a courtesy visit. He was in a hurry to leave.

'You have an excellent doctor. He studied under Martel. A pity that, for the rest—'

'The rest of what?'

'I know what I'm saying . . . Don't worry about it . . . I'll see you soon . . . I'll come by and inquire after you every day.'

Maigret ate his lemon curd, which was a pure masterpiece. But the aroma of truffles coming from the dining room was tantalizing.

'It's unbelievable!' said his wife. 'Here they serve truffles the way they serve potato salad elsewhere! Even with the fifteen-franc menu! Anyone would think they were cheap!'

And then it was Leduc's turn.

'Sit down. Some lemon curd? No? What do you know about the private life of my doctor, whose name I don't even know.'

'Doctor Rivaud! I don't know much. Gossip. He lives with his wife and his sister-in-law. The locals say that the sister-in-law is as much his wife as the other one . . . But—'

'What about the prosecutor?'

'Monsieur Duhourceau? Have you already heard?'

'Tell me anyway!'

'His sister, who's the widow of a master mariner, is mad. Rumour has it that he had her put away because of her fortune.'

Maigret was jubilant. His former colleague stared at him in horror as he sat up in bed screwing up his eyes to gaze out at the square.

'What else?'

'Nothing! In small towns—'

'Only, you see, my dear Leduc, this is not a small town like any other! It's a small town where there's a madman at large!'

The funniest part was that Leduc displayed a genuine anxiety.

'A madman at large! A madman who is only intermittently mad and who, the rest of the time, comes and goes and talks like you and me.'

'Your wife isn't too bored here?'

'She's turning the kitchens upside down! She gives the chef recipes and copies out the ones he gives her . . . After all, maybe it's the chef who's mad—'

There is something intoxicating about having escaped death and convalescing, being coddled, especially in such unreal surroundings.

And about exercising his brain in spite of everything, just for pleasure.

About observing a region, a town, from his bed, from his window . . .

'Is there a library here?'

'Of course there is!'

'Well, I'd be really grateful if you'd go and borrow all the books about mental illness, perversion, manias . . . and also bring me up the telephone directory. Very enlightening, the telephone directory! Ask them downstairs if their phone has a long cable and if it could be brought up to my room from time to time.'

Maigret was sleepy. He felt drowsiness rise in him like a fever and suffuse every fibre of his being.

'By the way, tomorrow you're having lunch here. It's Saturday—'

'And I have to buy a goat!' Leduc finished the sentence looking around for his straw hat.

When he left, Maigret's eyes were already closed and regular breaths were coming out of his half-open mouth.

Downstairs, the retired inspector ran into Doctor Rivaud. He took him to one side and dithered for a while before murmuring, 'Are you sure that this wound hasn't affected my friend's mind? At least his . . . I don't know how to put it . . . Do you follow my meaning?'

The doctor gave a dismissive wave.

'Is he usually a clever man?'

'Very clever! He doesn't always appear so, but—'

'Ah, ha!'

And the surgeon started up the stairs looking pensive.

3. The Second-class Ticket

Maigret had left Paris on the Wednesday afternoon. That night, he was shot just outside Bergerac. He spent Thursday and Friday at the hospital. On the Saturday, his wife arrived from Alsace, and she and Maigret settled into the spacious first-floor room at the Hôtel d'Angleterre.

On the Monday, Madame Maigret suddenly asked him, 'Why didn't you travel with your free train pass?'

It was 4 p.m. Madame Maigret, who could never sit still, was tidying the room for the third time.

The pale window blinds had been pulled down halfway, creating a luminous screen between the room and the square humming with life.

Maigret, puffing at one of the first pipes he'd been allowed, gazed at his wife in astonishment. She was pink with embarrassment and he had the impression that she was avoiding his eyes as she waited for his reply.

The question was ridiculous. He did indeed have a first-class pass, as did all the Flying Squad inspectors, enabling him to travel anywhere in France. He had used it on the journey from Paris.

'Come and sit down over here,' he muttered.

His wife hesitated. He almost forced her to sit down on the edge of the bed.

'Tell me!'

He looked at her mischievously and she became more flustered.

'I shouldn't have phrased the question like that. If I did, it's because at times you behave strangely,' she said.

'You think so as well, do you?'

'What do you mean?'

'I mean everyone here thinks I'm strange and they don't entirely believe my train story. And now—'

'Yes! Well, in the corridor earlier, I moved the doormat and I found this just outside our door.'

Although living in the hotel, Madame Maigret was wearing an apron, so as to feel 'a little more at home', as she put it. She fished a railway ticket from her pocket. It was a Paris–Bergerac second-class return, dated the previous Wednesday.

'Just outside our door,' repeated Maigret. 'Get a pencil and a piece of paper.'

Baffled, she did as he asked and moistened the lead.

'Write this down . . . First of all, the hotel owner, who came at around nine this morning to see how I was . . . Then the doctor, just before ten. Put the names in columns. The prosecutor dropped in at midday and the police inspector arrived as he was leaving.'

'And there's Leduc!' ventured Madame Maigret.

'Correct! Add Leduc! Is that everyone? Plus, of course, any one of the hotel staff or any traveller who could have dropped the ticket in the corridor.'

'No!'

'Why not?'

'Because the corridor only leads to this room! Unless it's someone who came to eavesdrop outside the door!'

'Get me the stationmaster on the phone!'

Maigret was not acquainted with the town, or the station, or any of the places people mentioned to him. And yet he had already built up a fairly accurate and almost complete mental picture of Bergerac.

A Michelin guide had provided him with a map of the town. And he was right in the centre of it. The square he could see was Place du Marché. The building to the right was the law courts.

The guide said:

Hôtel d'Angleterre. First-class. Rooms from twenty-five francs. Bathrooms. Set menus at 15 and 18 francs. Specialities: truffles, foie gras, stuffed chicken, Dordogne salmon.

The Dordogne river was behind Maigret, hidden from view. But he followed its course with the help of a set of postcards. Another card showed him the station. He knew that the Hôtel de France, on the other side of the square, was the Hôtel d'Angleterre's rival.

And he visualized the streets converging towards the main roads like the one he had stumbled along.

'The stationmaster's on the phone!'

'Ask him if any passengers got off the train from Paris on Thursday morning.'

'He says no!'

'That's all!'

Mathematically, it was almost certain that the ticket belonged to the man who had jumped on to the track just before Bergerac and who had shot the inspector!

'Do you know what you ought to do? Go and see the house of Monsieur Duhourceau, the prosecutor, and then the surgeon's.'

'Why?'

'No reason! So you can tell me what you have seen.'

Left on his own, Maigret relished the chance to smoke more pipes than he was permitted. Dusk was softly falling and the main square was all rosy. The commercial travellers returned from their rounds one by one, parking their cars on the strip in front of the hotel. From below came the thwack of billiard balls.

It was aperitif time in the bright hotel lounge and the owner, in his chef's hat, came in and glanced around from time to time.

Why did the man from the train risk his life and jump off before we reached the station, and why, when he realized he was being followed, did he shoot? In any case, the man was familiar with the line, since he had jumped on to the track at the precise moment when the train slowed down.

If he hadn't gone all the way to the station, it was because the staff knew him. But that wasn't sufficient to prove that he was the murderer of the Moulin-Neuf farm woman and the stationmaster's daughter.

Maigret remembered how restless his fellow passenger had been, his irregular breathing, the silences followed by sighs of despair.

'At this hour, Duhourceau must be at home, in his study, reading the Paris newspapers or consulting his files . . . The surgeon will be doing his ward round, followed by the nurse . . . The police inspector—'

Maigret was in no rush. Usually, at the start of an investigation, he was almost giddy with impatience. He couldn't stand uncertainty. He only calmed down when he felt he was getting close to the truth.

This time, it was the contrary, perhaps because of his condition.

Hadn't the doctor told him that he would have to stay in bed for about a fortnight and even then he would have to be very careful?

He had plenty of time. Long days to kill, piecing together a lifelike picture of Bergerac from his bed with all the characters in position.

'I'm going to have to ring for someone to come and put the light on!'

But he was so lazy that he didn't, and when his wife came back, she found him lying in pitch darkness. The window was still open, letting in the cool evening air. The street lamps formed a garland of light around the square.

'Do you want to catch pneumonia? Fancy leaving the window open when—'

'Well?'

'Well what? I saw the houses! I don't see what use it can be.'

'Tell me!'

'Monsieur Duhourceau lives on the other side of the law courts, on a square that's almost as big as this one. A large two-storey house. There's a stone balcony on the first floor. That must be his study, since there was a light on in the room. I saw a manservant closing the ground-floor shutters.'

'Is it cheerful?'

'What do you mean? It's a big house like any other big house! A bit gloomy . . . In any case, there are dark red velvet curtains that must have cost around two thousand francs per window. A soft, silky velvet that falls in big folds.'

Maigret was delighted. Little by little he adjusted his mental image of the house.

'The manservant?'

'What about the manservant?'

'Was he wearing a striped waistcoat?'

'Yes!'

And Maigret felt like clapping: a solid, austere house, with opulent velvet curtains, a dressed stone balcony, antique furniture! A manservant in a striped waistcoat! And the prosecutor in a morning coat, with grey trousers, patent-leather shoes and grey hair in a crew cut.

'You're right, he does wear patent-leather shoes!'

'Button-up shoes! I noticed them yesterday.'

The man from the train also wore patent-leather shoes, but did they have buttons? Or laces?

'What about the doctor's house?'

'It's right at the end of the town! A villa like a seaside home.'

'Like an English cottage!'

'That's it! With a low roof, lawns, flowers, a pretty garage, white gravel paths, green-painted shutters, a wrought-iron lantern. The shutters weren't closed. I got a peek at his wife, who was embroidering in the sitting room.'

'What about the sister-in-law?'

'She came home in the car with the doctor. She's very young, very pretty, very chic. You'd never know she lived in a small town, she must have her dresses sent from Paris—'

What connection could this have with a madman who attacked women on the road, strangled them and then plunged a needle into their heart?

Maigret didn't attempt to find an answer. He simply contented himself with placing people.

'You didn't meet anyone?'

'No one I know. People probably don't go out in the evening.'

'Is there a cinema?'

'I spotted one, in a sidestreet. It's showing a film that I saw in Paris three years ago.'

Leduc arrived at around ten, parked his old Ford outside the hotel and knocked a little later at Maigret's door. Maigret was drinking a bowl of broth that his wife had made in the kitchen.

'Is everything all right?'

'Sit down! No! Not in the sun. You're blocking my view of the square.'

Since Leduc had retired, he had grown rather stout. And there was something softer, more apprehensive about him than in the past.

'What's your cook making for your lunch today?' he asked.

'Lamb cutlets with cream sauce. I have to keep to a light diet. By the way, you haven't been to Paris recently, have you?' inquired Maigret.

Madame Maigret looked round abruptly, taken aback by this question out of the blue. And Leduc, seemingly disconcerted, gazed at his colleague reproachfully.

'What do you mean? You know very well that—'

Of course! Maigret knew very well that . . . but he was watching his colleague, who had a little auburn moustache. He looked at his feet encased in heavy hunting boots.

'Between ourselves, what do you do around here for love?'

'Stop that,' Madame Maigret broke in.

'Not at all! It's a very important question!' retorted Maigret. 'Here in the country you don't find all the conveniences of the city . . . Your cook, Leduc. How old is she?'

'Sixty-five! You can see that—'

'No others?'

The most embarrassing part was perhaps Maigret's seriousness in asking questions that would normally be voiced in a light or ironic tone.

'No little shepherdess in the area?'

'There's her niece, who sometimes comes to help out.'

'Sixteen? . . . Eighteen?'

'Nineteen. But—'

'And you . . . er—'

Leduc didn't know where to put himself and Madame Maigret, more embarrassed than he was, made herself scarce.

'You're tactless!'

'In other words, you have? . . . Well, my friend!'

And Maigret seemed to put the matter out of his mind. Then, a few moments later, he muttered, 'Duhourceau isn't married . . . Does—?'

'It's obvious that you come from Paris! You speak of these matters as if it were the most natural thing in the world. Do you think the prosecutor tells the whole world about his escapades?'

'But since everyone knows everyone else's business, I'm sure you know.'

'I only know what people say.'

'You see!'

'Monsieur Duhourceau goes to Bordeaux once or twice a week . . . and there—'

Maigret did not take his eyes off his friend and a strange smile hovered on his lips. He had known a different, less reserved Leduc, one who did not use such circumspect language or display provincial fears.

'Do you know what you should do, since you are able to come and go as you please? Start a little investigation to find out who was out of town last Wednesday. Hold on! I'm particularly interested in Doctor Rivaud, the prosecutor, the police inspector, yourself and—'

Leduc had risen to his feet, vexed. He looked at his straw hat as if he were about to put it on his head and leave.

'No! That's enough nonsense. I really don't know what's the matter with you. Since your injury, you . . . well, you've been behaving oddly! Can you really see me investigating the public prosecutor, in a little place like this where everything gets about? And the police inspector! When I no longer hold an official position! Not to mention that your insinuations—'

'Sit down, Leduc!'

'I haven't got much time.'

'Sit down, I tell you, and you'll understand. Here, in Bergerac, there's a man who, in his everyday life, has all the appearances of a normal man and probably has a profession. He's a man who, suddenly, in a fit of madness—'

'And you're lumping me in with the possible murderers! Do you think I didn't get the drift of your questioning? Your need to know whether I had any mistresses . . . Because you're thinking that a man who is starved is more likely to lose control—'

He was very angry. His face was red, his eyes glinted.

'The prosecutor's office is handling this case, and so are the local police! It's none of my business! Now, if you want to meddle in—'

'—things that don't concern me! Too bad! But now suppose that in one or two days' time, or three or eight, your nineteen-year-old girlfriend is found with a needle stuck in her heart—'

Leduc would hear no more. He snatched his straw hat and rammed it on his head so hard that it split. Then he stomped out, slamming the door behind him.

That was the signal Madame Maigret had been waiting for. She came back in, nervous, worried.

'What has Leduc done to you? I've rarely seen you be so nasty to someone. Anyone would think you suspect him of—'

'Do you know what you should do? He'll be back later, or tomorrow, and I'm convinced he'll apologize for his rude exit. Well, I'm going to ask you to go and have lunch with him tomorrow, at La Ribaudière—'

'Me? But—'

'Now, please will you fill a pipe for me and plump up my pillows?'

Half an hour later, when the doctor came in, Maigret gave a delighted smile and hailed Rivaud cheerfully.

'What did he say to you?'

'Who?'

'My colleague Leduc . . . He's worried! He must have asked you to give me a thorough mental examination. No, doctor, I'm not mad. But—'

He was cut off in mid-sentence as the doctor placed a thermometer under his tongue. While he was taking Maigret's temperature, he removed the dressing from his wound, which was slow to heal.

'You're moving around too much! . . . Thirty-eight point seven . . . I don't need to ask if you've been smoking, the air in here is thick.'

'You should ban him completely from smoking his pipe, doctor!' said Madame Maigret.

But her husband broke in, 'Can you tell me how long it was between the murders committed by our madman?'

'Wait a minute . . . The first took place a month ago . . . The second, one week later . . . Then the failed attempt, the following Friday and—'

'Do you know what I think, doctor? That there's a strong chance that we're on the eve of a new attack. Or rather, I'd say, if it doesn't happen, it's because the murderer knows he's being watched, and if it does—'

'Well?'

'Well! We can proceed by elimination. Supposing that at the time of the murder, you're in this room. That's you in the clear! Supposing that the prosecutor is in Bordeaux, the police inspector in Paris or elsewhere, my friend Leduc wherever the hell—'

The doctor stared at the patient.

'In short, you're restricting the field of possibilities—'

'No! Of probabilities.'

'Same thing! You're restricting it, I say, to the little group you saw when you came round after the operation—'

'Not exactly, since I'm forgetting the clerk! I'm restricting it to the people who visited me at some point yesterday and who could have accidentally dropped a railway ticket. By the way, where were you last Wednesday?'

'Last Wednesday?'

And the doctor, disconcerted, searched his memory. He was a young, active, ambitious man, with precise gestures and an elegant appearance.

'I think that . . . Wait . . . I went to La Rochelle to—'

But he bristled at the inspector's amused smile.

'Is this an interrogation? If it is, I warn you—'

'Calm down! Remember I have nothing to do all day,

and I'm used to leading an intensely active life. So I make up little games to play on my own. The madman game! There's nothing to prevent a doctor from being mad, or a madman from being a doctor. It's even said that psychiatrists are nearly all their own patients. There's no reason either why a public prosecutor shouldn't—'

And Maigret heard the doctor quietly ask his wife, 'He hasn't had anything to drink, has he?'

The best moment was after Doctor Rivaud had left. Madame Maigret went over to the bed, frowning her disapproval.

'Do you know what you're doing? Really! I don't understand you! If you want people to think you're mad, you're going the right way about it! The doctor didn't say anything . . . He's too polite . . . but I could tell that . . . Why are you grinning like that?'

'Nothing! The sunshine! The red-and-green-striped wallpaper . . . The women prattling in the square . . . The little lemon-yellow car that looks like a fat beetle . . . and the smell of foie gras . . . Only the thing is, there's a madman . . . Look at that pretty young woman walking past, with the lovely plump calves of a mountain girl. She has tiny pear-shaped breasts . . . Maybe she's the one who the madman will—'

Madame Maigret looked him in the eyes and realized he wasn't joking any more, that he was being utterly serious, and there was sorrow in his voice.

He took her hand and concluded, 'I'm convinced this isn't over! And with all my heart I would like to make sure that a beautiful girl who's alive and well today, doesn't cross this square one of these days in a hearse, escorted by people in mourning. There's a madman in the town, in the sunshine! A madman who talks, laughs, who comes and goes—'

And in a cajoling voice, he muttered, his eyes half-closed, 'Let me have a pipe. Please!'

4. A Gathering of Madmen

Maigret had chosen his favourite time of day, 9 a.m., because of the rare quality of the light at that hour and also the signs of life in the main square – a door being opened by a housewife, the clatter of cart wheels, a shutter suddenly flung open – which would continue intensifying until midday.

From his window, he could see on the trunk of a plane tree one of the posters he'd had put up all over the town.

Wednesday at 9 a.m., Hôtel d'Angleterre, Inspector Maigret will be offering a reward of 100 francs to any person bringing him information about the attacks in Bergerac, which appear to be the work of a madman.

'Should I stay in the room?' asked Madame Maigret who, even though in a hotel, managed to be as busy as in her own home.

'You can stay!'

'I'm not too keen! Anyway, no one will come.'

Maigret smiled. It was only 8.30 and, lighting his pipe, he cocked his head at the sound of an engine and murmured, 'Here's one already!'

It was the familiar sound of the old Ford that could be heard as soon as it drove up to the bridge.

'Why didn't Leduc come yesterday?'

'We exchanged a few words. We don't exactly see eye-to-eye over the madman. All the same, he'll be here shortly!'

'The madman?'

'Leduc . . . The madman too! . . . And perhaps even several madmen! . . . It's a question of probability . . . An advert like that has an irresistible appeal for all the unhinged, the over-imaginative, the highly strung, the epileptics . . . Come in, Leduc!'

Leduc hadn't even had the time to knock at the door. He looked a little awkward.

'Weren't you able to come yesterday?'

'No, I wasn't . . . Please forgive me . . . Good morning, Madame Maigret . . . I had to go and fetch the plumber because of a leaky pipe . . . Are you feeling better?'

'I'm fine! . . . My back's still as stiff as a board, but otherwise . . . Did you see my poster?'

'What poster?'

He was lying. Maigret nearly told him so, but decided to spare him that cruelty.

'Sit down! Give your hat to my wife. In a few minutes, we're going to have some visitors. And I'd stake my life on the madman being among them.'

There was a knock at the door. And yet nobody had crossed the square. A moment later, the hotel owner entered.

'I'm sorry . . . I didn't know you had a visitor . . . It's about the poster—'

'Do you have something to tell me?'

'Me? . . . No! . . . What are you thinking of! . . . If I'd had something to say, I'd already have said it . . . I simply wanted to know if we should allow everyone who turns up to come up to your room.'

'Yes! Yes of course!'

And Maigret looked at him through the lashes of his half-closed eyes. It was becoming an obsession with him, narrowing his eyes like that. Or was it perhaps because he was obstinately living in a ray of sunlight?

'You may leave us.'

And turning to Leduc, 'He's a strange character too! Powerful, sanguine, strong as a tree trunk, with a pink skin that always looks as if it's about to burst—'

'He's a former local farm lad, who started off by marrying his boss. He was twenty and she was forty-five.'

'And since then?'

'This is his third marriage! A fateful coincidence! They all die.'

'He'll be back later.'

'Why?'

'That I don't know! But he'll be back, when everyone's here. He'll find some excuse. Right now, the prosecutor is probably leaving his house, already wearing his morning coat. As for the doctor, I'll wager he's racing through his morning ward round to get it over with as fast as possible.'

The words were barely out of Maigret's mouth when Monsieur Duhourceau appeared at the end of a street and crossed the square with hurried steps.

'That makes three!'

'What do you mean, three?'

'The prosecutor, the owner and you.'

'Again? Now look here, Maigret—'

'Sssh! Go and open the door to Monsieur Duhourceau, who's loath to knock—'

'I'll be back in an hour!' announced Madame Maigret, putting on her hat.

The prosecutor greeted her ceremoniously and shook Maigret's hand without looking at him directly.

'I have been informed of your experiment. I wanted to see you beforehand. Firstly, it is understood that you are acting in a private capacity. Even so, I would like to have been consulted, given that there is an investigation under way—'

'Please sit down. Leduc, take Monsieur Duhourceau's hat and stick. I was just saying to Leduc that the murderer is bound to be here shortly . . . Good! Here's the inspector, who's looking at the time and will go and have a drink downstairs before coming up.'

He was right! They saw the inspector enter the hotel, but he didn't appear at the bedroom door for another ten minutes. He seemed taken aback to find the prosecutor there, apologized and stammered, 'I thought it my duty to—'

'Leduc! Get some chairs, will you! There must be some in another room . . . Here come our customers, only no one wants to be the first.'

Three or four people were indeed wandering around the square darting frequent glances in the direction of the hotel. You could see they were trying to compose themselves. Their eyes all lighted on the doctor's car as it pulled up right outside the entrance.

Despite the spring sunshine, there was tension in the air. The doctor, like his predecessors, looked put out to find so many people already gathered.

'Looks like a court martial,' he sniggered.

And Maigret noted that he was ill-shaven and his tie was not so neatly knotted as usual.

'Do you think that the investigating magistrate—'

'He's gone to Saintes to question a suspect and won't be back before this evening.'

'What about his clerk?' asked Maigret.

'I don't know if he's taken him with him . . . Or rather . . . Oh look, there he is coming out of his house. He lives on the first floor of that house with blue shutters just opposite the hotel.'

The sound of several people's footsteps on the stairs. Then whispers.

'Open the door, Leduc.'

This time it was a woman, one who had not come from outside. It was the maid who had almost been a victim of the madman's and who still worked at the hotel. A man came in behind her, shy and self-conscious.

'This is my fiancé, who works at the garage. He didn't want me to come because he says the less people talk about it—'

'Come in! . . . You too, fiancé . . . and you too, monsieur.'

For the hotel owner was on the threshold, his white chef's hat in his hand.

'I simply wanted to know whether my chambermaid—'

45

'Come in! Come in! What about you, what is your name?'

'Rosalie, monsieur . . . Only I don't know whether, for the reward . . . Because, I've already told everything I know, haven't I?'

And the fiancé, furious, muttered without looking at anyone, 'It had better be true!'

'Of course it's true! I wouldn't have made it up.'

'And you didn't make up the story of the guest who wanted to marry you either? And that time you told me that your mother had been brought up by gypsies?' he snapped.

The girl was angry, but she did not get flustered. She was a strong, thickset farm girl with powerful hips and shoulders. Whenever she moved, her hair became tousled, as if after a battle. As she stretched up to smooth it she revealed damp armpits with auburn tufts.

'It's like I said . . . I was attacked from behind and I felt a hand close to my chin. So I bit it as hard as I could. I even noticed he had a gold ring on his finger.'

'You didn't see the man?'

'He ran off into the woods straight away. He had his back to me and I was struggling to get up, given that—'

'So you wouldn't be able to recognize him! That's what you said in your statement?'

Rosalie clammed up, but there was something threatening in her obstinate expression.

'Would you recognize the ring?'

And Maigret's gaze wandered over all the hands. He looked at Leduc's pudgy hands, with their signet rings, at the doctor's long, tapering fingers, with only a wedding band, and the very pale hands with brittle skin of the prosecutor, who had pulled a handkerchief out of his pocket.

'It was a gold ring!'

'And you have no idea who your attacker could have been?'

'Monsieur, I assure you—' began the fiancé, his forehead beaded with sweat.

'Speak!'

'I don't want there to be any trouble. Rosalie is a good girl, and I say so to her face. But every night she dreams. Sometimes she tells me her dreams. Then a few days later, she believes that they really did happen. It's the same with the novels she reads.'

'Fill a pipe for me, would you, Leduc.'

Beneath the window, Maigret could now see a group of a dozen or so people conferring in low voices.

'So, Rosalie, you must have some idea—'

The girl said nothing. Only her gaze rested for a moment on the prosecutor, and once again Maigret saw the button-up patent-leather shoes.

'Give her a hundred francs, Leduc. Forgive me for using you as my secretary . . . Are you pleased with her, as her boss?' he asked the hotel owner.

'As a chambermaid I can't fault her.'

'Fine! Show in the next people.'

The clerk had slipped into the room and was standing with his back to the wall.

'I didn't know you were here. Do have a seat.'

'I don't have much time,' murmured the doctor, taking his watch out of his pocket.

'Bah! It'll be plenty.'

And Maigret lit his pipe, watched the door open to admit a young man dressed in rags, with tow-coloured hair and gummy eyes.

'I hope you're not going to—' muttered the prosecutor.

'Come in, my boy! When did you have your last fit?'

'He came out of hospital a week ago!' said the doctor.

He was obviously an epileptic, the archetypal 'village idiot'.

'What do you have to tell me?'

'Me?'

'Yes, you! Tell me.'

But, instead of speaking, the young man began to cry, and after a few minutes his sobs became convulsive. He might be about to have a fit. Those gathered could make out a few stammered words.

'I'm always the one who . . . I haven't done anything! . . . I swear it! . . . So why can't I be given a hundred francs to buy myself a suit?'

'A hundred francs! Next!' Maigret said to Leduc.

The prosecutor was growing visibly impatient. The police inspector had adopted a detached attitude and he commented, 'If the local police proceeded in the same manner, you can be sure that at the next council meeting—'

In a corner, Rosalie and her fiancé were having a whispered argument. The hotel owner poked his head out of the half-open door to listen to the noises from the ground floor.

'Do you really hope to find out something?' sighed Monsieur Duhourceau.

'Me? . . . Nothing at all.'

'In that case—'

'I promised you that the madman would be here and it is likely that he is.'

Only three more people came in: a roadmender who three days earlier had seen 'a shadow dodging in and out between the trees' which had fled at his approach.

'The shadow didn't do anything to you?'

'No!'

'And you didn't recognize him? OK, you can have fifty francs!'

Maigret was the only one to remain cheerful. In the square stood at least thirty townsfolk, in groups, staring up at the hotel windows.

'What about you?'

A shy-looking elderly farmer wearing mourning stood waiting.

'I am the father of the first woman who died. And I have come to say that if I get my hands on that monster, I'll—'

And he too tended to look at the prosecutor rather than Maigret.

'You have no idea?'

'An idea, maybe not! But I speak my mind, I do! Nothing can hurt a man who has lost his daughter! You'd do better to sniff around where things have already happened. I know you're not from around here . . . you don't know . . .

Everyone will tell you that things went on and no one ever found out what really happened.'

The doctor had risen, his impatience having got the better of him. The police inspector looked away, like a man who didn't want to hear, while the prosecutor remained inscrutable.

'Thank you, my good man.'

'And I don't want your fifty or your hundred francs. If you can come to the farm one day . . . Anyone will tell you where it is.'

He didn't ask whether he should stay. He didn't say goodbye but left, his shoulders hunched.

His departure was followed by a long silence and Maigret put on a show of being very busy tamping the ashes in his pipe with his good hand.

'A match, Leduc.'

There was something moving in this silence. And it was as if the scattered clusters of people in the square too were avoiding making the slightest sound.

Nothing but the elderly farmer's steps on the gravel.

'Please shut up, will you?'

It was Rosalie's fiancé who found himself speaking out loud and the girl stared straight ahead of her, possibly cowed into submission, possibly reluctant.

'Well, gentlemen,' Maigret sighed at last, 'it seems to me that things aren't going so badly.'

'We've already interviewed all these people!' retorted the inspector, rising and looking for his hat.

'Except that this time, the madman is in the room!'

Maigret did not look at anyone as he spoke, but stared at the white counterpane on his bed.

'Doctor, do you think that he remembers what he has done once his fits are over?'

'Almost certainly.'

The hotel owner was standing in the centre of the room, conspicuous in his chef's whites, which made him all the more self-conscious.

'Leduc, go and see if there are any more people waiting!'

'You'll excuse me, but I really have to leave now,' said Doctor Rivaud. 'I have an appointment at eleven and that too is a matter of a man's life.'

'I'll come with you,' mumbled the police inspector.

'What about you, monsieur?' Maigret asked the prosecutor.

'Um . . . I . . . Yes . . . I—'

For a few moments, Maigret had seemed dissatisfied and several times he glanced impatiently in the direction of the square. Suddenly, just as everyone was on their feet about to leave, he sat up slightly in bed and muttered, 'At last! One moment, gentlemen, I think we have something new.'

And he pointed to a woman running towards the hotel. The surgeon could see her from where he stood, and he said in amazement, 'Françoise!'

'Do you know her?'

'She's my sister-in-law. A patient must have telephoned me . . . or there's been an accident.'

Someone was running up the stairs. There were voices. The door opened and a young woman, panting, burst into the room and looked about her in terror.

'Jacques! Inspector! Monsieur Duhourceau—'

She wasn't more than twenty. She was slim, pretty, nervous.

But there was dust on her dress. Her bodice was partly torn. She kept touching her neck with her hands.

'I . . . I saw him . . . and he att—'

No one moved. She was struggling to speak. She took two steps towards her brother-in-law.

'Look!'

She showed him bruising on her neck, then continued, 'Over there . . . in the Moulin-Neuf woods . . . I was walking when a man—'

'I told you we'd learn something!' muttered Maigret who was back to his placid self.

Leduc, who knew him inside out, looked at him in amazement.

'You saw him, didn't you?' continued Maigret.

'Not for long! I don't know how I managed to shake him off. I think he tripped over a tree stump. I took advantage to hit him—'

'Can you describe him?'

'I don't know. A vagrant probably . . . dressed like a farmer . . . Big sticking-out ears . . . I've never seen him before.'

'Did he run away?'

'He realized I was about to scream . . . There was the

sound of a car on the road . . . He ran off into the bushes.'

She gradually got her breath back, keeping one hand on her neck, the other on her breast.

'I was so frightened . . . Perhaps, if it hadn't been for the sound of a car . . . I ran all the way here.'

'Excuse me, but weren't you closer to the villa?'

'I knew only my sister was at home.'

'Was it to the left of the farm?' asked the police inspector.

'Just past the disused quarry.'

And the inspector said, addressing the prosecutor, 'I'm going to have the woods searched. Perhaps it's not too late?'

Doctor Rivaud seemed vexed. Frowning, he watched his sister-in-law, who was leaning on the table, breathing more regularly.

Leduc sought Maigret's gaze and, when he met it, did not conceal his irony.

His look seemed to be saying, 'In any case, this seems to prove that the madman isn't here among us.'

The police inspector went downstairs and turned right towards the town hall, heading for the police station. The prosecutor slowly brushed his bowler hat with the back of his sleeve.

'As soon as the investigating magistrate comes back from Saintes, mademoiselle, I'll ask you to go to his chambers to repeat your story and sign a statement.'

He held out a dry hand to Maigret.

'I presume you no longer need us!'

'Naturally! I had not expected that you would take the trouble—'

Maigret signalled to Leduc, who understood that he must get everyone to leave. Rosalie and her fiancé were still arguing.

When Leduc came back to the bed, a smile on his lips, he was surprised to see his friend wearing a stern, anxious expression.

'Well?'

'Nothing!'

'It didn't work?'

'It worked too well! Fill a pipe for me, would you, while my wife's still out.'

'I thought the madman was supposed to come this morning.'

'That's right!'

'But—'

'Don't press me. What would be terrible, you see, would be if another woman were murdered. Because, this time—'

'What?'

'Don't try to understand. Right! There's my wife crossing the square. She's going to tell me I smoke too much and she'll hide my tobacco. Slip a little under the pillow—'

He was hot. Perhaps he was even slightly flushed.

'Off you go! Leave the telephone by my bed.'

'I plan to have lunch at the hotel. It's goose confit today. I'll drop in and say hello this afternoon.'

'If you like. By the way, that girl . . . You know, the one

you told me about . . . How long is it since . . . since you last saw her?'

Leduc bristled, looked his friend in the eye and complained, 'That's going too far!'

And he went out, leaving his straw hat on the table.

5. The Patent-leather Shoes

'Yes, madame . . . At the Hôtel d'Angleterre . . . Obviously it is entirely up to you if you prefer not to come—'

Leduc had just left. Madame Maigret was on her way up the stairs. The doctor, his sister-in-law and the prosecutor were standing in the square, beside Rivaud's car.

Maigret was telephoning Madame Rivaud, who must have been alone at home. He asked her to come to the hotel, and was not surprised to hear an anxious voice on the other end of the line.

Madame Maigret overheard the end of the conversation as she took off her hat.

'Is it true that there's been another attack?' she asked. 'I met some people rushing over to the Moulin-Neuf.'

Absorbed in thought, Maigret didn't answer. He saw the activity in the town gradually change. The news spread quickly and more and more people were converging on a path that began to the left of the square.

'There must be a level crossing!' muttered Maigret, who was beginning to know the town's layout.

'Yes! There's a long road that starts out as a street and turns into a dirt track. The Moulin-Neuf is after the second bend. These days, there's no windmill but a big farmhouse with white walls. When I walked past, they were harnessing the oxen, in a farmyard full of poultry. There were some fine turkeys—'

Maigret listened like a blind man hearing a description of a landscape.

'Is there a lot of land?'

'Here, they measure in *journaux*. I was told 200 *journaux*, but I don't know how much that is. In any case, the woods begin straight away. Further on, you come to the main road to Périgueux.'

The gendarmes were probably there, and the few police officers from Bergerac. Maigret pictured them striding through the undergrowth, as on a rabbit hunt. And the clusters of people on the road, the kids clambering up the trees.

'You should leave me alone now. Go back there, would you?'

She didn't argue. On her way out, she walked past a young woman entering the hotel and turned around in surprise, with perhaps a hint of irritation.

It was Madame Rivaud.

'Please sit down. And forgive me for having brought you here, especially for such a trifling matter. For I'm not even sure I have any questions to ask you! This business is so muddled.'

Maigret did not take his eyes off her and she sat there mesmerized by his gaze.

The inspector was surprised, but not bewildered. He'd had a hunch that Madame Rivaud would be of interest to him and he could see that she was a much more curious character than he had dared hope.

Her sister Françoise was slim and elegant, giving not the slightest hint that she was from the country or a small town.

Madame Rivaud was much less striking and was not even what might be described as a pretty woman. She was between twenty-five and thirty, of average height and slightly plump. Her clothes were made by a local seam-stress, or, if they did come from a good fashion house, she didn't know how to wear them.

Her most striking feature was her anxious, tormented eyes. Worried and at the same time resigned.

For example, the way she looked at Maigret, he could tell she was frightened, but that she was incapable of react-ing. It would barely be an exaggeration to say she was waiting to be beaten.

Very petty bourgeois. Very *proper*! Fidgeting absently with a handkerchief with which she could dab at her eyes if necessary.

'Have you been married long, madame?'

She did not reply immediately. The question scared her. Everything scared her.

'Five years,' she breathed at last in a neutral voice.

'Were you already living in Bergerac?'

And once again she stared at Maigret for a long while before answering.

'I lived in Algeria, with my sister and my mother.'

He was afraid to continue, so conscious was he that the slightest ill-judged word was likely to frighten her off.

'Did Doctor Rivaud live in Algeria?'

'He worked at Algiers Hospital for two years.'

Maigret looked at the young woman's hands. There was something incongruous about them compared with her bourgeois outfit. Those hands had worked. But it would be awkward to shift the conversation on to that territory.

'Your mother—'

He trailed off. She sat facing the window and now she was getting to her feet, a look of terror on her face. There was the sound of a car door slamming below.

Doctor Rivaud got out of his car, ran into the hotel and knocked furiously on the door.

'You're here?'

He said this to his wife, in a sharp tone, without looking at Maigret, then he turned to the inspector.

'I don't understand . . . You need my wife? . . . In which case, you could have—'

She bowed her head. Maigret watched Rivaud with mild surprise.

'Why are you angry, doctor? I wished to make Madame Rivaud's acquaintance. Unfortunately I'm unable to get up and about and—'

'Is the interrogation over?'

'It is not an interrogation, but a quiet conversation. When you came in, we were talking about Algeria. Do you like that country?'

Maigret's sang-froid was an act. Staring at the two people in front of him, he spoke slowly and deliberately while mustering all his energy. Madame Rivaud seemed on the verge of tears, and Rivaud cast about him as if looking for traces of what had happened and trying to understand.

There was something hidden. Something was amiss.

But where? What?

There had been something amiss with the prosecutor too. Only it was all confused, muddy.

'Tell me, doctor, did you meet your wife while she was your patient?'

Rivaud glanced quickly at Madame Rivaud.

'Believe me, that is of no importance. With your permission, I'll drive my wife home and—'

'Of course. Of course—'

'Of course what?'

'Nothing! . . . Excuse me! . . . I wasn't even aware that I was speaking out loud . . . It's a strange case, doctor! Strange and alarming. The further I get, the more alarming I find it. Your sister-in-law, on the other hand, was very quick to regain her composure after receiving such a fright earlier. She's a very spirited person!'

And he saw Rivaud freeze, feeling uneasy, waiting for what was to come next. Wasn't the doctor convinced that Maigret knew a lot more than he was letting on?

The inspector felt he was making progress, but suddenly, everything was turned upside down, the theories he was elaborating, the life of the hotel and of the town.

It began with the arrival of a gendarme on a bicycle in the square. He rode around a block of houses, heading for the prosecutor's home. Just then, the telephone rang and Maigret answered.

'Hello, this is the hospital. Is Doctor Rivaud still with you?'

Nervously the doctor took the receiver, listened with

astonishment, hung up, so emotional that he just stood there for a moment staring into space.

'They've found him,' he said at last.

'Who?'

'The man! . . . At least, a body . . . in the Moulin-Neuf woods.'

Perplexed, Madame Rivaud gazed from one to the other.

'They want to know if I can carry out the autopsy. But—'

Struck by a thought, now it was his turn to look at Maigret suspiciously.

'When you were attacked . . . it was in the woods . . . you fought back . . . You fired at least once.'

'I didn't fire.'

And another idea dawned on the doctor, who feverishly wiped his hand across his forehead.

'He's been dead several days . . . but then, how come Françoise . . . this morning—?' Turning to his wife, he said, 'Come—'

He and his wife departed, she meekly allowing herself to be led. Shortly afterwards he could be seen bundling her into his car. Meanwhile, the prosecutor must have telephoned for a taxi, for there was one drawing up outside his house. And the gendarme pedalled off again.

By now, the town's initial curiosity had intensified and reached fever pitch. Soon, everybody, including the hotel owner, was making their way to the Moulin-Neuf and only Maigret stayed behind in bed, his back straight, his heavy gaze fixed on the sun-warmed square.

*

'What's wrong?'

'Nothing.'

As Madame Maigret came back into the room, she could only see her husband's profile, but she realized from his fierce stare that something was the matter. It didn't take her long to guess and she went over and sat on the edge of the bed, mechanically picked up the empty pipe and set about filling it.

'Don't worry . . . I'll try and give you all the details . . . I was there when they found him and the police allowed me to go up close.'

Maigret was still gazing out of the window but, as she spoke, it was other images than those of the square that were imprinted on his retina.

'That section of the woods is on a slope . . . There are oak trees beside the road . . . Then it's a pine wood . . . People arrived by car and parked on the bend, on the verge . . . The gendarmes from a neighbouring village encircled the woods so as to surround the man . . . The ones from here advanced slowly and the old farmer from Moulin-Neuf was with them, a regulation revolver in his hand . . . No one dared say anything to him . . . I think he'd have shot the murderer.'

Maigret pictured the woods, the ground carpeted with pine needles, the dappled light and shade, the gendarmes' uniforms.

'Suddenly, a kid running alongside the group screamed and pointed to a shape lying at the foot of a tree.'

'Patent-leather shoes?'

'Yes! And hand-knitted grey wool socks. I looked closely, because I remembered—'

'How old?'

'Around fifty, maybe. It's hard to know exactly. He was lying face down. When they turned him over, I had to look away because . . . you understand! . . . Apparently he's been there for at least a week . . . I waited for them to cover his face with a handkerchief . . . I heard people saying that in any case, no one recognizes him. He's not from around these parts.'

'Any injuries?'

'A big hole in his temple . . . and when he fell, he must have got a mouthful of earth as he lay dying.'

'What are they doing now?'

'The local bigwigs are on the way. The police are keeping the public out of the woods. When I left, they were waiting for the prosecutor and Doctor Rivaud. Then the body will be taken to the hospital for the autopsy.'

The square was emptier than Maigret had ever seen it.

The sole presence was a little café-au-lait coloured dog lying in the sunshine.

Midday tolled, slowly. Men and women workers spilled out of a printing works in a neighbouring street and made a beeline for the Moulin-Neuf, most of them on bicycles.

'How was he dressed?'

'In black, with a straight overcoat. It's hard to say because of the state in which—'

Madame Maigret felt sick, but all the same, she asked, 'Do you want me to go back there?'

★

Maigret was left alone. The hotel owner returned, shouting up to him from the street, 'Have you heard? . . . To think I've got to come back and get on with my lunches!'

And silence, the blue sky, the square golden in the sunlight, the empty houses.

It was not until an hour later that Maigret heard the clamour of a crowd coming from a nearby street: it was the body being brought to the hospital escorted by the entire town.

Then the hotel filled up. The square grew lively. Downstairs, glasses clinked. There was a timid knock at the door and Leduc appeared, giving a tremulous smile.

'May I come in?'

He sat down beside the bed and lit his pipe before speaking.

'So that's it!' he sighed.

He was astonished, when Maigret turned towards him, to see a smiling face, and above all to hear, 'Well, are you happy?'

'But—'

'And all of them! The doctor! The prosecutor! The inspector! All delighted with the prank that's been played on the nasty policeman from Paris! He was wrong all along! He thought he was so clever, he put on such airs that at one point people were about to take him seriously and some were even quaking in their shoes.'

'You have to admit that—'

'That I was wrong?'

'The man's been found! And the description matches the one you gave us of the stranger on the train. I saw him.

A middle-aged individual, rather shabbily dressed, although with a certain studied elegance. Someone had put a bullet through his brain, almost at close range, as far as we can tell given the state of—'

'Yes!'

'Monsieur Duhourceau agrees with the police that he committed suicide, around a week ago, perhaps immediately after attacking you.'

'Was the gun found beside his body?'

'That's just it! Not exactly. They found a gun in his overcoat pocket which was missing just one bullet.'

'Of course! Mine!'

'That's what we need to try and establish . . . If he committed suicide, the case becomes easier . . . Knowing he was being hunted, about to be caught, he—'

'What if he didn't commit suicide?'

'There are several plausible explanations . . . A farmer could have been attacked by him in the night and shot him . . . Then, afterwards, been afraid of complications – that's how country folk are.'

'What about the attack on the doctor's sister-in-law?'

'They discussed that too. It's possible that a prankster simulated an attack and—'

'In other words, everybody wants to wash their hands of the whole business!' sighed Maigret, exhaling a puff of smoke that rose up in the shape of a halo.

'That's not entirely true! But it's clear that there's no point dragging things out and that once—'

Maigret laughed at his colleague's discomfiture.

'There's still the railway ticket,' he said. 'Someone will

have to explain how that ticket got from our stranger's pocket into the corridor of the Hôtel d'Angleterre.'

Leduc stared stubbornly at the crimson rug and suddenly he blurted out, 'Do you want a piece of advice?'

'Leave all this alone! Get better as soon as I can and leave Bergerac.'

'And come and spend a few days at La Ribaudière, as we planned! I spoke to the doctor about it and he said that if we're careful, we could take you there now.'

'And what does the prosecutor have to say about that?'

'I don't understand.'

'He must have put his oar in too. Did he not remind you that I have absolutely no business in getting involved in this case, except as victim?'

Poor Leduc! He wanted to be kind. He was trying to placate everyone at the same time. And Maigret was doggedly persistent!

'You have to admit that officially—'

And suddenly, taking the bull by the horns, Leduc said, 'Look, I'd rather be honest. After your nonsense this morning, you're certainly not very popular around here. The prosecutor has dinner every Thursday with the prefect and he told me earlier that he's going to have a word with him about you, to ensure that you receive orders from Paris. There's one thing that has particularly annoyed them, and that's the handing out of hundred-franc notes. They're saying—'

'That I want to encourage the dregs of the population to spill the beans—'

'How do you know?'

'. . . that I'm listening to malicious insinuations and that in short I'm stirring up ill feeling . . . Phew!'

Leduc said nothing. He had no answer. Deep down, he agreed with Maigret. A few minutes later, he timidly ventured, 'If only you had an actual lead! In that case, I must say I'd change my mind and that—'

'I don't have any leads! Or rather I have four or five. This morning, I had hoped that at least two of them would get me somewhere. Well, they didn't. They fizzled out on me!'

'You see! . . . And another mistake, perhaps one of the most serious, because you've made yourself a vicious enemy . . . The idea of telephoning the doctor's wife! . . . He's so jealous that few people can claim to have ever seen her! . . . He barely allows her out of the house.'

'And yet he is Françoise's lover! Are you saying he's jealous of one and not of the other?'

'That's none of my business. Françoise comes and goes. She even drives around on her own in the car. As for his lawful wife . . . In short, I heard Rivaud tell the prosecutor that he considered your behaviour as boorish and that he had a strong urge to teach you some manners.'

'Sounds promising!'

'What do you mean?'

'That he's the one who changes my dressing and checks my wound three times a day!'

And Maigret laughed, too heartily and too noisily for it to be sincere.

He laughed like someone who has put themselves in a ridiculous situation and is determined to carry on, because it is too late to back down, but has no idea how to extricate himself.

'Aren't you going to have lunch? I recall you saying something about goose confit.'

And Maigret laughed again! There was a thrilling game to be played! There were things to be done everywhere – in the woods, in the hospital, at the Moulin-Neuf farm, at the doctor's and perhaps in the prosecutor's austere house with curtains – absolutely everywhere, and goose confit to be eaten, and poached truffles, and a whole town that Maigret hadn't even seen!

He was confined to a bed, a window, and he wanted to scream every time he made a sudden movement! He had to ask someone to fill his pipe for him because he was unable to use his left arm, and Madame Maigret was taking advantage of the situation to put him on a diet!

'Will you accept my invitation?' asked Leduc.

'When all this is over, I promise.'

'But now that the madman is dead!'

'Are we sure? Go and have lunch! If anyone asks what my plans are, say you don't know! And now, to work!'

He said that exactly as if he were faced with a crushing material task, such as kneading dough, or turning over tons of earth.

And he did indeed have a lot of things to turn over: a jumbled, inextricable heap.

But they were not tangible things: he was haunted by faces, some of them quite hazy – the prosecutor's surly, superior expression, the doctor's anxious look, the sad, careworn face of his wife, who had been his patient in

Algiers Hospital – what had been wrong with her? – Françoise's highly strung and overly assertive demeanour . . . and Rosalie, who dreamed every night, much to her fiancé's despair – were they actually sleeping together already? And that insinuation concerning the prosecutor – that there were things that had been hushed up! And what about the man who'd jumped from the moving train only to shoot at Maigret and die? Leduc and his cook's niece – very risky, that! The hotel owner, who had already had three wives – but had the temperament to do away with twenty!

Why had Françoise—?

Why had the doctor—?

Why had secretive Leduc—?

Why? Why? Why?

And they wanted to get rid of Maigret by packing him off to La Ribaudière?

He gave one last laugh, the laugh of a big man. And when his wife came in a quarter of an hour later, she found him sleeping blissfully.

6. *The Seal*

Maigret was having an exhausting dream. He was by the sea. It was excessively hot and the tide was out, exposing the sand, which was the russet colour of ripe corn. There was more sand than sea, which was present, somewhere, a long way away, but there was nothing on the horizon except little pools between the sand banks.

Was Maigret a seal? Perhaps not exactly! But he wasn't exactly a whale either! He was a very large, very round, gleaming black animal.

He was alone in this torrid expanse. And he was aware that at all costs he somehow had to reach the sea, where he would be free at last.

Except that he was unable to move. He had little stumps like a seal but he didn't know how to use them. They were all stiff. When he raised himself up, he slumped heavily on to the sand, which scorched his back.

He absolutely had to reach the sea, otherwise, he'd get stuck in the sand into which he sank deeper and deeper with every movement.

Why was he so stiff? Had he been wounded by a hunter? He couldn't remember. And he turned round and round on the spot. He was in a pitiful state – a big, black, sweating heap.

★

When he opened his eyes, the sunlight was already streaming in through the oblong window and he saw his wife sitting at a table having breakfast, looking at him.

From this first glance, he knew something was amiss. It was a look he knew well, too solemn, too maternal, with a hint of anxiety.

'Were you in pain?'

His second sensation was that his head was heavy.

'Why do you ask that?'

'You were tossing and turning all night. Several times you groaned.'

She rose and came over to kiss him.

'You're pale,' she added. 'You must have had a nightmare.'

Then he remembered the seal and was torn between a gnawing disquiet and an urge to laugh. But he didn't laugh. It was all connected. Madame Maigret, sitting on the edge of the bed, said softly, as if she were afraid of upsetting him, 'I think we need to make a decision.'

'A decision?'

'I spoke to Leduc, last night. It's clear that you would be better at his place where you'll be able to rest and recover fully.'

She didn't dare look him in the eye. He knew all that and murmured, 'You too?'

'What do you mean?'

'You think I'm wrong, don't you? You're convinced I won't succeed and that—'

That was enough for perspiration to appear at his temples and above his top lip.

'Calm down! The doctor's coming and—'

It was time for the doctor's visit. Maigret hadn't seen him since the previous day's scene and the prospect of their conversation banished his anxieties for the moment.

'I want you to leave me alone with him.'

'And we'll go and stay at Leduc's?'

'We won't be leaving here. That's his car pulling up. Off you go now.'

Doctor Rivaud usually took the stairs three at a time, but that morning he made a more dignified entrance, curtly waving a greeting to Madame Maigret, who was on her way out. He put his bag down on the bedside table without saying a word.

The morning visit always followed the same routine. Maigret put the thermometer in his mouth while the surgeon removed his dressing.

They did as usual and it was during the ritual procedure that the conversation took place.

'Naturally,' began the doctor, 'I will carry out my duty towards you as an injured man to the end. But I shall simply ask you to accept that from now on, our relationship will stop there. Furthermore, please note that given that you have no official business here, I forbid you to harass members of my family.'

It sounded like a rehearsed speech. Maigret did not respond. He was bare-chested. The doctor removed the thermometer from his mouth and he heard him mutter, 'Still thirty-eight!'

That was high, he knew. The doctor frowned and, avoiding his gaze, went on, 'Had it not been for your attitude yesterday, I would say to you, as a doctor, that the best thing you can do is to finish convalescing in a quiet place. But that advice could be misinterpreted and . . . Does that hurt?'

As he spoke, he was probing the wound, where there were still infected areas.

'No . . . Carry on.'

But Rivaud had nothing more to say. The visit continued in silence, and it was in silence too that the surgeon put away his instruments and washed his hands. Only as he was leaving did he look directly at Maigret.

Was it a physician's look? Was it the look of Françoise's brother-in-law, or of the curious Madame Rivaud's husband?

In any case, it was a look that contained anxiety. Before going out, he almost spoke. But he chose to hold his tongue and only on the stairs were there whisperings between him and Madame Maigret.

The worst thing was that now the inspector recalled all the details of his dream. And he felt other warnings. He hadn't said anything earlier, but the examination had been much more painful than the day before, which was worrying. So was this persistent fever. So worrying that having picked up his pipe from the bedside table, he put it down again.

His wife came in, sighing.

'What did he say to you?' asked Maigret.

'He didn't want to say anything! It was me who questioned him. I gather he recommended complete rest.'

'How far has the official investigation got?'

Madame Maigret sat down, resigned. But her entire manner showed that she disapproved of her husband, that she did not share his obstinacy or his confidence.

'The autopsy?'

'The man must have died within a few hours of having attacked you.'

'They still haven't found the weapon?'

'Nothing! The photograph of the body is in all the newspapers this morning, since no one knows who he is. It's even in the Paris papers.'

'Show me.'

And Maigret took the newspaper with a certain emotion. As he looked at the photograph, he was aware that he was the only person who had actually known the dead man.

He hadn't seen him, but they had spent a night together. He recalled his travelling companion's agitated sleep – was it really sleep? – his sighs, and his sobbing.

Then the two dangling legs, the patent-leather shoes and hand-knitted socks.

The photograph was gruesome, like all photographs of corpses that have been touched up to look lifelike so as to make identification easier.

An insipid face. Glazed eyes. And Maigret was not surprised to see a grey beard eating into his cheeks.

Why had he already thought that on the train? He had never imagined his fellow passenger other than with a grey beard!

And he did have one, or rather there were hairs three centimetres long sprouting all over his face.

'In truth, this case is none of your business!'

His wife was back on the attack, gently apologetic. She was very concerned about Maigret's state of health. She

gazed at him the way people look at someone who is seriously ill.

'Yesterday in the restaurant I overheard people talking.
They are all against you. You can question them but no
one will tell you what they know. If that's the case—'

'Would you pick up a pen and a piece of paper?'

He dictated a telegram to an old friend of his at the
Algiers criminal investigation department.

*Please cable urgently to Bergerac all information concerning
junior doctor named Rivaud, Algiers Hospital, five years ago.
Thank you. Regards. Maigret.*

His wife's face spoke volumes. She wrote as instructed,
but she did not believe in this investigation. She did not
have faith.

And he could tell. He fumed. He allowed scepticism in
others. But in his wife, it was intolerable. He was so riled
that he lost his temper, or rather spoke scathingly.

'There! No need for you to correct it, or give me your
opinion! Send that telegram! Find out how the investigation is progressing! I'll do the rest.'

She looked at him as if to ask him to make peace, but
he was already too angry.

'What's more, I would ask you to keep your opinions
to yourself in future! In other words, no need to confide
in the doctor, in Leduc, or in any other imbecile!'

He turned over, so heavily, so clumsily, that he felt like
the seal in his nightmare.

★

His writing was laboured, which made the letters thicker than usual. He breathed noisily, because his position was uncomfortable. Two kids were playing marbles just beneath his window, and he had to keep fighting the urge to yell at them to stop.

> *First crime: the Moulin-Neuf farmer's daughter-in-law is attacked on the path, strangled and then stabbed in the heart with a long, thin needle.*

He sighed and noted in the margin:

> *(time, exact place, strength of the victim?)*

He knew nothing! In an ordinary investigation, these details would not have been difficult to establish. Currently, it was a right to-do.

> *Second crime: the stationmaster's daughter is attacked, strangled and stabbed in the heart with a needle.*
> *Third crime (aborted): Rosalie is attacked from behind, but she fights off her attacker, who flees.*
> *(Dreams every night and reads novels. Fiancé's testimony.)*
> *Fourth crime: a man who jumps off a moving train and whom I chase shoots me, injuring me in the shoulder. Note that this takes place in the Moulin-Neuf woods, like the three other incidents.*
> *Fifth crime: the man is killed by a bullet through his brain, in the same woods.*

Sixth crime (?): Françoise is attacked, in the Moulin-Neuf woods, and gets the better of her assailant.

He screwed up the sheet of paper and threw it away, shrugging. He took another, and wrote in a casual hand:

Duhourceau: mad?
Rivaud: mad?
Françoise: mad?
Madame Rivaud: mad?
Rosalie: mad?
Inspector: mad?
Hotel owner: mad?
Leduc: mad?
Stranger with patent-leather shoes: mad?

But actually, why was there a need for anyone to be mad? Maigret suddenly furrowed his brow, remembering his first hours in Bergerac.

Who was it that had spoken to him of madness? Who had insinuated that the two crimes could only have been committed by a madman?

Doctor Rivaud!

And who had immediately agreed? Who had pointed the official investigation in that direction?

Duhourceau, the prosecutor!

And suppose they stopped looking for a madman? Suppose they simply looked for a logical explanation for the chain of events?

For example, might not the sole purpose of the needle through the heart be to make people believe that the murders were the work of a sadist?

On another sheet, Maigret wrote the title: *Questions*. And he doodled around the letters like an idle schoolboy.

1. *Was Rosalie really attacked or was it only in her imagination?*
2. *Was Françoise attacked?*
3. *If she was, was it by the same killer who attacked the first two women?*
4. *Was the man in grey socks the killer?*
5. *Who killed the killer?*

Madame Maigret returned, gave a cursory glance over at the bed, crossed the room to remove her hat and coat and finally came and sat beside her husband.

With a mechanical gesture, she took the pages and the pencil from him and sighed, 'Dictate!'

For a moment, he was torn between the temptation to consider this attitude as a challenge, an insult, and create another scene, and the need to relent and make peace with his wife.

He looked away, awkward as he always was in these situations. She skimmed over the lines he had written.

'Have you got an idea?'

'Nothing at all!' he exploded. No, he didn't have any ideas! No, he couldn't make head or tail of this wantonly complicated story. He fumed. He was on the point of giving up. He wanted to rest, to go and spend the few remaining days of his holiday at Leduc's little manor house, surrounded by chickens and the soothing sounds of the farmyard, the smell of cows and horses.

But he didn't want to back down. He didn't want any advice.

Did she finally understand? Was she really going to help him, instead of stupidly nagging him to rest?

That is what his misty eyes asked her.

And she replied with a phrase she didn't often use, 'My poor Maigret!'

She only called him Maigret in certain circumstances, when she recognized that he was the man, the master, the strength and the brains of the household. Perhaps this time she didn't say it with a great deal of conviction. But he anxiously awaited her reply like a child in need of encouragement.

There, now he had it.

'Give me another pillow, would you?'

No more silly emotion, little outbursts of temper, childishness.

'And fill me a pipe!'

The two kids in the square were arguing. One of them got a smack in the face and ran straight into a low house, began to cry the minute he was inside and complained to his mother.

'Before we do anything else, we need a schedule. I think it's best to act as if we don't expect to receive any new information. In other words, to work with what we've got and try out all the different theories until one of them rings true.'

'I ran into Leduc in town.'

'Did he speak to you?'

'Of course!' she said with a smile. 'He entreated me again to persuade you to leave Bergerac and stay at his place. He was coming out of the prosecutor's house.'

'Well! Well!'

'He spoke volubly, like a man who is worried.'

'Did you go to the mortuary to see the body again?'

'There is no mortuary. They've put him in the lockup. Fifty people were crowding around the door. I waited for my turn.'

'Did you see the socks?'

'Good-quality wool. Hand-knitted.'

'Which suggests a man whose life is organized or who, at the very least, has a wife, a sister or a daughter who takes care of him. Or again he could be a vagrant! For vagrants are given socks knitted in convents by girls from good families.'

'Except that vagrants don't travel in sleeper compartments.'

'Nor, generally, do tradespeople, and even less minor officials. At least in France. The sleeper suggests someone who is used to long journeys. What about the shoes?'

'You can see the brand. They are sold in a hundred or two hundred branches.'

'The suit?'

'A very worn black suit, but of good cloth, which was made to measure. It has been worn for at least three years, like the overcoat.'

'The hat?'

'It hasn't been found. The wind must have blown it away.'

Maigret thought back but couldn't remember if the man from the train had a hat.

'Did you notice anything else?'

'His shirt collar and cuffs had been darned. Rather neatly done.'

'Which seems to indicate that a woman looked after this man. Wallet, documents, anything in his pockets?'

'Nothing but a very short ivory cigarette holder.'

They spoke simply, naturally, like two old colleagues. They were relaxing after hours of exasperation. Maigret smoked his pipe, giving out little puffs.

'Here's Leduc!'

They saw him cross the square, his bearing more ungainly than usual, his straw hat tipped back slightly. When he reached the landing, Madame Maigret opened the door to him and he forgot to greet her.

'I've just been at the prosecutor's.'

'I know.'

'Yes . . . your wife told you . . . Then I dropped by the police station to check that the news was true. This is completely unheard of! Devastating.'

'What?'

Leduc mopped his face. He absent-mindedly drank half a glass of lemonade that had been made for Maigret.

'Do you mind? . . . It's the first time such a thing has happened . . . Naturally they sent the fingerprints to Paris! . . . They've just received the reply . . . Well!'

'Well?'

'Our corpse has been dead for years!'

'You're saying—?'

'I'm saying that officially, our corpse has been dead for years. He's a certain Meyer, known as Samuel, sentenced to death in Algiers and—'

Maigret had raised himself up on his elbows.

'And executed?'

'No! He died in hospital a few days before his execution!'

Madame Maigret could not help giving an affectionate, slightly mocking smile at the sight of her husband's jubilant face.

He caught her smile, and nearly smiled back. His dignity prevailed and he put on an appropriately solemn expression.

'What had Samuel done?'

'Paris doesn't say. We only received a coded telegram. We'll have a copy of his record this evening. Don't forget that Bertillon himself recognized that there's one chance in a hundred thousand, if I'm not mistaken, that the fingerprints of two different people could be identical. There's always the possibility that we've come across the exception.'

'Is the prosecutor peeved?'

'Of course he's annoyed. Now he's talking about calling in the Flying Squad. But he's afraid of ending up with inspectors who'll come to get their instructions from you. He asked me if you were very influential at HQ and so on.'

'Fill me a pipe!' Maigret said to his wife.

'This is the third one!'

'It doesn't matter. I bet my temperature isn't even thirty-seven now! Samuel! The comfortable shoes! Samuel is Jewish. Jews usually have sensitive feet. They also have strong family ties – hence the knitted socks. And they're thrifty – the three-year-old suit in heavy-duty cloth.'

He interrupted himself.

'I'm joking, my friends! But to tell you the truth, I have just spent a wretched few hours! Just the thought of that dream . . . Now, at least, the seal – unless the seal is a whale! – the seal, I say, has set off . . . and you'll see how it goes on its merry way.'

He burst out laughing, because Leduc was looking at Madame Maigret with alarm.

7. Samuel

The two items of news arrived more or less at the same time just before the surgeon's evening visit.

First of all a telegram from Algiers:

Doctor Rivaud unknown hospitals. Regards. Martin.

Maigret had barely opened it when Leduc came in. He didn't dare ask his colleague what he was reading.

'Look at this!'

Leduc glanced at the dispatch, shook his head and sighed, 'Of course!', meaning, 'Of course we can't expect anything to be straightforward in this case! At every turn we encounter new obstacles! And I'm right to insist that the best thing is for you to come and settle comfortably at La Ribaudière.'

Madame Maigret had gone out. Even though it was getting dark, Maigret did not think to turn on the light. The street lamps in the square were lit and at that hour, he liked looking out at the garland of evenly spaced lights. He knew that the house where the lights would go on first was the second one past the garage and he would then be able to make out the shape of a seamstress under the lamp, always hunched over her work.

'The police have received some news too!' muttered Leduc.

He was ill at ease. He didn't want it to look as though he had come to inform Maigret. Perhaps he had even been asked not to keep the inspector abreast of the progress of the official investigation.

'News of Samuel?'

'Correct! First of all, they've received his record. Then Lucas, who had dealt with him in the past, telephoned from Paris to give details.'

'And?'

'No one knows exactly where he's from. But there is good reason to believe that he was born in Poland, or in Yugoslavia. Somewhere around there, in any case. A taciturn man, who didn't talk openly to people about his business. He had an office in Algiers. Guess what he did?'

'Some tedious specialist activity, I'm sure!'

'Stamp dealer!'

And Maigret was thrilled, because that fitted perfectly with the individual from the train.

'A stamp business that was a front for something else, of course! The best part is that it was so clever that the police weren't aware of it and it took a double murder before . . . I'm repeating pretty much what Lucas said on the telephone. The office in question was one of the biggest operations producing fake passports and above all false employment contracts. Samuel had accomplices in Warsaw, Vilnius, Silesia, Constantinople—'

By now the night was inky blue. The houses stood out pearly white against the sky. From downstairs came the usual pre-dinner hum of conversation.

'Strange!' said Maigret.

It was not so much Samuel's occupation that he found strange, but the realization that threads that once stretched between Warsaw and Algiers led to the little provincial town of Bergerac. And it was stranger still that a purely local case, a small-town crime, should be connected to the international criminal world.

People like Samuel, he had come across countless times in Paris and elsewhere, and he had always studied them with a curiosity mixed with disquiet, not exactly repulsion, as if they were of a different species from ordinary human beings. They might be barmen in Scandinavia, American gangsters, managers of gambling clubs in Holland or elsewhere, headwaiters or theatre directors in Germany, merchants in North Africa, and so on.

There, in the tranquillity of Bergerac's idyllic square, was a reminder of a frightening world, terrifying in its power, its vastness and its tragic fate. Central and Eastern Europe, from Budapest to Odessa, from Tallinn to Belgrade, teeming with an over-populous humanity . . . Hundreds of thousands of starving Jews leaving each year and heading in all directions. Ocean liners' holds crammed with migrants, night trains, babes in arms, elderly parents in tow, resigned, tragic faces filing past the frontier posts.

Chicago has more Poles than Americans . . . France had taken in trainloads and trainloads, and, in villages, the town-hall registrars had to ask people to spell out their names when they came to register births or deaths.

There were all the official exiles, with their papers in order, and there were the others, who didn't have the patience to wait their turn, or who could not obtain a visa.

And that's where the Samuels stepped in! Samuels who knew every village of origin and every destination, every frontier station, every consulate stamp and every official's signature.

Samuels who spoke ten languages and as many dialects.

And who camouflaged their activity behind a prosperous business, international if at all possible.

Postage stamps, clever!

Mr Levy, Chicago,
I shall be sending you by the next steamship two hundred rare stamps, orange vignette, from Czechoslovakia.

And, of course, like most of his fellow operators, Samuel must have trafficked not only men!

In the special establishments in South America, it was the French girls who were the pick of the bunch. Those who sent them worked in Paris, on the Grands Boulevards.

But the bulk of the troupe, the cheap goods, came from Eastern Europe. Peasant girls who left at the age of fifteen or sixteen and returned at twenty – or didn't return at all – after earning their dowry.

All that was daily fodder at Quai des Orfèvres.

What bothered Maigret was this Samuel's sudden appearance in the Bergerac case in which, until that point, there had only been Duhourceau the prosecutor, the doctor and his wife, Françoise, Leduc, the hotel owner . . .

The intrusion of a disturbing new world, with a dramatically new atmosphere—

In other words, the entire case took on a different

complexion. Maigret could see into a tiny grocer's shop opposite his window, and by now he knew every single jar on the shelves. A little further was the garage's petrol pump, which must have been purely decorative because petrol was still sold in cans!

Leduc was saying, 'Another brainwave was to have set up the operation in Algeria . . . As a matter of fact, Samuel had a large Arab clientele and even Africans.'

'His crime?'

'Two crimes! Two men of his race, unknown in Algiers, who were found dead on a patch of waste ground. They had both come from Berlin. Inquiries were made. It emerged that they had both worked with Samuel for many years. The investigation went on for months. They couldn't find any evidence. Samuel fell ill and had to be transferred from the prison infirmary to the hospital.

'The police more or less pieced together the story: the two Berlin associates had come to complain of irregularities. Samuel must have been a shrewd operator who cheated everyone. They turned nasty—

'And our man did away with them!'

'He was sentenced to death. But he was never executed because he died in hospital a few days after the verdict. That's all I know!'

The doctor was surprised to find the two men sitting in the dark and it was he who snapped on the light. Then he put his bag down on the table, and after a curt greeting removed his spring overcoat and started running hot water in the washbasin.

'I'm off!' said Leduc, rising. 'I'll see you tomorrow.'

He could not have been thrilled to have been caught in Maigret's room by Rivaud. He was a local, and it was in his interest to keep both sides happy, since now there were two opposing camps.

'Take care of yourself! Goodbye, doctor!'

And the doctor, who was soaping his hands, replied with a grunt.

'Your temperature?'

'So-so!' retorted Maigret.

He felt cheerful, as at the beginning of the whole business, when it had been such a joy for him to feel that he was still alive.

'The pain?'

'Bah! I'm getting used to it.'

There was a daily routine, always the same, that had become a sort of ritual. While this took place, Rivaud's face was constantly very close to that of Maigret, who suddenly said, 'You don't have very pronounced Jewish features!'

No reply, other than the regular, slightly wheezy breathing of the doctor, who was probing the wound. When it was done, the dressing back in place, he declared, 'You are now fit to travel.'

'What do you mean?'

'That you are no longer a prisoner in this hotel room. Weren't you supposed to be going to stay with your friend Leduc for a few days?'

The man had perfect self-control, and that was a fact! For at least a quarter of an hour, Maigret had been staring fixedly at him but he hadn't uttered a word, delicately attending to the patient's wound with steady hands.

'From now on, I shall only come every other day and I'll send you my assistant to change the dressing. You can have complete confidence in him.'

'As much as in you?'

There were moments – very few! – when Maigret was not able to resist blurting out a snide remark like that, with a naive air that gave it all its piquancy.

'Good night!'

And he was gone! Maigret was alone once more with all the characters in his head, plus the famous Samuel who, from the outset, had led the parade.

A Samuel who had the ultimate and unique characteristic of having died twice!

Was he the murderer of the two women, the madman with the needle?

In which case, there were already puzzling questions, two at least: first of all, why had he chosen Bergerac as his theatre of operations?

People of that kind prefer cities, where the population is more mixed and they have a better chance of going unnoticed.

But Samuel had never been seen in Bergerac, or in the entire region, and with his patent-leather shoes, he clearly wasn't a man to live in the woods like a cartoon bandit.

Did that mean that someone had been harbouring him under their roof? The doctor? Leduc? Duhourceau? The Hôtel d'Angleterre?

Secondly, the Algiers murders were planned, clever

crimes with the aim of eliminating accomplices who had grown dangerous.

The Bergerac murders, on the other hand, were the work of a madman, a sex maniac or a sadist.

Had Samuel gone mad between the first murders and the second? Or, for some subtle reason, had he felt the need to feign madness, using the needle as a sinister cover?

'I'd be curious to know whether Duhourceau has ever been to Algeria!' muttered Maigret.

His wife came back, exhausted. She flung her hat on to the table and sank into the wing chair.

'What a profession you've chosen!' she sighed. 'To think you rush around like this all the time—'

'Any news?'

'Nothing of interest. I heard that the report on Samuel has arrived from Paris. It's being kept hush-hush.'

'I know about it.'

'Leduc? That's nice of him since you're still not very popular around here. People are confused and anxious. There are some who claim that the Samuel business has nothing to do with the madman's murders, that he's simply a man who came and committed suicide in the woods and that sooner or later another woman will be killed.'

'Did you go for a stroll past Rivaud's villa?'

'Yes! I didn't see anything, but I did find out a tiny little thing that might be of no importance. On a couple of occasions a woman of a certain age, quite common-looking, came to the villa. She is thought to be the doctor's mother-in-law. But no one knows where she lives or whether she's still alive. Her last visit was two years ago.'

'Pass me the telephone!'

And Maigret asked for the police station.

'Is that the secretary? . . . No, don't bother to disturb the chief . . . Just tell me Madame Rivaud's maiden name. I don't suppose you have any objection.'

A few moments later he smiled. Covering the mouthpiece with his hand, he said to his wife, 'He's gone to call the inspector to ask if he can give me the information! They don't know what to do! They'd love to say no. Hello! . . . Yes . . . Beausoleil, you said? . . . Thank you.'

He hung up and said, 'A splendid name! And now, I'm going to give you a painstaking job! You're going to go through the telephone directory and make a list of all the medical schools in France. Then you will call each one and ask if a degree was awarded, some years ago, to a certain Rivaud.'

'You think he won't be . . . But . . . but then, since he's the one who's looking after you—'

'Go on!'

'Do you want me to phone from the telephone booth downstairs? I realized that people in the dining room can hear everything that's being said.'

'Exactly!'

And he was left alone once more. He filled a pipe and closed the window, as the air was turning chilly.

It took no effort for him to picture the doctor's villa, the prosecutor's gloomy house.

He who so enjoyed going out and sniffing atmospheres!

That of the villa must surely be one of the strangest. A simple decor, with clean lines. One of those houses that arouses envy in passers-by who say to themselves, 'How happy they must be in there!'

They see light-filled rooms, beautiful curtains, flowers in the garden, gleaming brass . . . The car purrs at the garage door . . . A slim young woman slides behind the wheel, or it's the dapperly dressed surgeon . . .

What could the three of them have to talk about in the evenings? Did Madame Rivaud know about her sister and her husband's love affair?

She wasn't pretty, and she knew it. There was nothing of the sweetheart about her, she looked more like a resigned housewife.

And there was Françoise, bursting with life!

Did they keep it secret to protect her? Did they exchange furtive kisses behind closed doors?

Or was the situation out in the open? Maigret had seen a similar set-up once before, in a house that was much more austere in appearance. And that was in the countryside too!

Who were these Beausoleils? Was the story about Algiers Hospital true?

In any case, in those days, Madame Rivaud must have been a little country girl. There were numerous little tell-tale signs, certain looks, certain gestures, a tiny detail in her bearing and the way she dressed.

Two little country girls . . . The eldest, who was more *striking*, still betrayed her origins even after many years.

The youngest, on the other hand, had adapted much better and was able to create the illusion that—

Did they hate each other? Did they confide in each other? Were they jealous of each other?

What about their mother, Madame Beausoleil, who had come to Bergerac twice? For some reason, Maigret pictured a fat country dweller delighted to have got her daughters off her hands, advising them to be nice to such an important and wealthy gentleman as the surgeon.

They probably gave the mother a little allowance.

'I can just imagine her in Paris, in Montmartre, or better still, in Nice.'

Did they discuss the murders over dinner?

Oh, to pay them a visit, just one, for only a few minutes! Look at the walls, the knick-knacks, the trifling objects that clutter every home, revealing so much of a family's private life.

To visit Monsieur Duhourceau's house too! For there was a connection, perhaps extremely tenuous, but there was one!

They formed a clan. They supported each other!

On an impulse, Maigret rang down and asked the hotel owner to come up. And he asked him outright, 'Do you know whether Monsieur Duhourceau often dines at the Rivauds'?'

'Every Wednesday. I know because he doesn't want to take his own car and it's my nephew who chauffeurs him and—'

'Thank you!'

'Is that all?'

The owner left, bemused. And around the imaginary table with its white tablecloth, Maigret placed another guest – the public prosecutor, who was probably seated on Madame Rivaud's right.

'And it was a Wednesday, or rather during the night of

Wednesday to Thursday, that I was attacked when I jumped off the train and Samuel was killed!' it suddenly dawned on him.

So they had dined together at the doctor's. Maigret had the feeling he had taken a giant stride forwards. He picked up the telephone receiver.

'Hello! The Bergerac exchange? This is the police, mademoiselle—'

He spoke in a booming voice, for he was afraid his request would be refused.

'Would you tell me if last Wednesday, Doctor Rivaud received a telephone call from Paris?'

'I'll check his account.'

It didn't take a minute.

'He received a call at two o'clock from Archives one-four-six-seven—'

'Do you have a list of the Paris subscribers classified by phone number?'

'I think I've seen one somewhere. Would you hold on?'

A pretty girl, for certain! And cheerful! Maigret smiled as he spoke to her.

'Hello? . . . I've found it. It's the Quatre Sergents restaurant, Place de la Bastille.'

'A three-minute call?'

'No, three units! That means nine minutes.'

Nine minutes! At two o'clock in the afternoon! The train had left at three! That night, while Maigret was travelling in the overheated compartment, beneath the bunk of his insomniac fellow passenger, the prosecutor had been having dinner at the Rivauds' house.

Maigret felt wildly impatient, and all but leaped out of bed. He sensed he was close to the end but this was not the time to make a mistake.

The truth was there, somewhere, within his grasp. It was now just a matter of intuition, of interpreting the facts he possessed.

Except that, at those moments, there's a danger of rushing headlong down the wrong track.

'Let's think . . . They are at the table . . . What was Rosalie insinuating against Monsieur Duhourceau? . . . Probably an ardour that is inappropriate in a man of his age and social status . . . In small towns, you can't tickle a little girl under the chin without being called a dirty old man . . . And did Françoise—? She was the type of woman to arouse a man of a certain age . . . So, they're at dinner . . . In the train, Samuel and myself . . . and Samuel is already afraid . . . For it's a fact that he's afraid . . . He's trembling . . . He has difficulty breathing—'

Maigret was drenched. He could hear the waitresses downstairs clattering plates.

Did he jump from the moving train *because he thought he was being followed or because he knew someone was waiting for him?*

Maigret realized that was a crucial question. He had touched on a sensitive point. He repeated softly, as if someone were going to reply, '. . . *because he thought he was being followed or because he knew someone was waiting for him?*'

Now, the telephone call—

His wife came in, so flustered that she didn't notice Maigret's excitement.

'We have to call a doctor right away, a real one! It's preposterous! It's a crime! When I think—'

And she looked at him as if searching for worrying scars on his face.

'He isn't qualified! He's not a doctor! He isn't listed on any register. Now I understand why you had a temperature of forty that went on and on and your wound refuses to heal.'

That's it! Maigret was jubilant. *It's because he knew someone was waiting for him!*

The telephone rang. The hotel owner was on the line: 'Monsieur Duhourceau is asking if he can come up!'

8. A Book Collector

Maigret's expression was transformed instantly, becoming neutral, glum and resigned, like that of any sick person bored out of their mind.

Perhaps because of that, the atmosphere in the room also changed. It was oppressive, with the unmade bed that had been moved, the newer-looking floorboards in the oblong where a rug had been, medicines on the bedside table and Madame Maigret's hat left casually lying about.

As if by chance, Madame Maigret had just lit a small spirit stove to make herb tea.

The overall effect was a little depressing. There was a brisk rap at the door. Madame Maigret let in the prosecutor, who inclined his head then automatically handed her his walking stick and hat, and went over to the bed.

'Good evening, inspector.'

He wasn't too ill at ease. He looked more like a man who had psyched himself up to fulfil a set task.

'Good evening, Monsieur Duhourceau. Please sit down.'

And, for the first time, Maigret saw a smile on the prosecutor's furrowed face. A parting of the lips! It was rehearsed too!

'I almost felt remorse because of you . . . That surprises you? . . . Yes, I was annoyed at myself for having been a little too harsh towards you . . . It is true that your attitude is sometimes aggravating—'

He sat with his hands resting flat on his thighs, his body leaning forwards, and Maigret looked straight at him with round eyes that seemed to be vacant of any thoughts.

'In short, I've decided to bring you up to date on—'

The inspector could certainly hear him, but he would have been incapable of repeating anything the prosecutor said. He was, in fact, minutely studying his attributes, both physical and moral.

A very light complexion, almost too light, which his grey hair and moustache only served to emphasize . . . Monsieur Duhourceau did not have liver disease . . . He was neither ruddy nor gouty.

Where was his weak spot? A man doesn't reach the age of sixty-five without something going wrong!

'Hardening of the arteries!' replied Maigret to himself.

And he stared at the thin fingers, the hands with silky skin but bulging veins as hard as glass.

A small, thin man, tense, intelligent, hot-tempered!

And morally, where was his weak spot, what was his vice?

He had one! Maigret could sense it! Beneath the prosecutor's dignity, there was something nebulous, elusive, shameful.

Monsieur Duhourceau was talking, '. . . in two or three days' time, at the most, the investigation will be over . . . The facts speak for themselves! . . . How Samuel managed to elude death and have another person buried in his stead is a matter for the Algiers prosecutor's office, if they are inclined to rake over this old story . . . In my view, it will be out of the question—'

At times his voice dropped slightly and he would look into Maigret's eyes, only to be met with a blank stare. Then he wondered whether the inspector was listening to him, whether he should interpret this absence as supreme irony.

He made an effort, his voice grew steadier.

'The fact remains that this Samuel, who was perhaps already not quite right in the head when he lived over there, arrives in France, hides out all over the place and soon goes completely mad . . . That sort of thing frequently happens, as Doctor Rivaud will tell you . . . He commits his crimes . . . In the train, he thinks you are on to him . . . He shoots at you, then becomes increasingly panic-stricken and ends up committing suicide.'

The prosecutor added, with a wave that was much too casual, 'By the way, I don't attach much importance to the absence of the gun by the body . . . There are hundreds of similar cases in the crime annals . . . A prowler could have passed by, or a child . . . and it will come to light in ten years' time, or twenty . . . The main thing is that the shot was fired at fairly close range and the autopsy will confirm that. So in a nutshell—'

Meanwhile, Maigret repeated to himself, 'What is his vice?'

Not drink! Not gambling! And, strangely, the inspector was tempted to add, 'Not women either!'

Miserliness? That was already more plausible! It was easier to imagine Monsieur Duhourceau behind closed doors opening his safe and setting out wads of notes and little bags of gold on the table.

In fact, he rather gave the impression of a loner! Whereas gambling is a shared vice! As is love! And drink nearly always—

'Monsieur Duhourceau, have you ever been to Algeria?'

'Me?'

When someone answers *me* in that way, it is invariably to play for time.

'Why are you asking me that? Do I look like a colonial? No, I have never been to Algeria, nor even to Morocco. The furthest I have travelled was to visit the Norwegian fjords. That was in 1923.'

'Yes . . . I really don't know why I asked . . . you have no idea how weak losing all that blood has made me.'

Another old trick of Maigret's: jumping from one subject to another and suddenly talking about things that have nothing to do with the conversation.

The other person, fearing a trap, tries to guess at an ulterior motive when there isn't one. They make an intense effort of the imagination, become frustrated, tired, and end up losing their train of thought.

'That's what I was telling the doctor. By the way, who does the cooking at their house?'

'What—'

But Maigret didn't give him time to reply.

'If it's one of the two sisters, it's certainly not Françoise! It's easier to imagine her at the wheel of a fast car than watching over a stew on the stove . . . Would you be so kind as to pass me that glass of water?'

And Maigret, raised up on one elbow, began to drink, but so clumsily that he dropped the glass, spilling its contents on to Monsieur Duhourceau's leg.

'I'm sorry! . . . How stupid of me! My wife will wipe it off straight away. Luckily water doesn't stain.'

The prosecutor was furious. The water had soaked through his trousers and must have been dribbling down his leg.

'Don't trouble yourself, madame . . . As your husband says, it doesn't stain. It really doesn't matter.'

He said this with irony.

Maigret's words, and now this little incident on top of things, had dispelled his earlier good humour and his sense of being in control. He was on his feet. He remembered that he still had other things he wanted to say.

But now he was not playing his part well, and could only manage to sound relatively cordial.

'What about you, inspector, what are your intentions?'

'Still the same!'

'Meaning?'

'To apprehend the killer, of course! And then, if I still have some leave left, to go and stay at La Ribaudière, where I should have been for the last ten days.'

Monsieur Duhourceau was incensed. What? He had taken the trouble to pay Maigret this visit and tell him all he'd told him, practically wooed him, and then, after spilling a glass of water on his leg – and the prosecutor was convinced that Maigret had done it deliberately! – he calmly announced, 'I'm going to apprehend the killer!'

He dared say that to him, the prosecutor, at the very moment when he had just stated that there was no more killer! Did that not sound like a threat? Should he storm out again, slamming the door behind him?

Monsieur Duhourceau managed a smile.

'You're stubborn, inspector!'

'You know, when one's lying in bed all day with nothing else to do . . . You wouldn't happen to have any books you could lend me, would you?'

Another probing question. And Maigret definitely had the impression that the prosecutor was looking ruffled.

'I'll send you some.'

'Cheerful books, please.'

'It's time for me to leave.'

'My wife will bring you your hat and stick. Are you dining at home?'

And he extended his hand to the prosecutor, who did not dare refuse it. Once the door had closed behind him, Maigret remained absolutely still, gazing at the ceiling, and his wife began, 'Do you think that—?'

'Is Rosalie still working at the hotel?'

'I think I saw her on the stairs.'

'You must get her for me.'

'And people will carry on saying—'

'It doesn't matter!'

While he waited, Maigret said to himself, 'Duhourceau is afraid! He's been afraid all along! Afraid that the killer will be found and afraid that his private life will be revealed! Rivaud is afraid too. Madame Rivaud is afraid—'

What remained was to establish what connection there could be between these people and Samuel, exporter of poor wretches from Central Europe and master document forger!

The prosecutor was not Jewish. Rivaud could be, but it wasn't certain.

The door opened and Rosalie entered, followed by Madame Maigret. She wiped her coarse red hands on her linen apron.

'Monsieur asked for me?'

'Yes, my dear . . . Come in . . . Sit down here.'

'We're not allowed to sit down in the rooms!'

She sounded anxious, she was afraid of getting into trouble. This wasn't the chatty, friendly girl of before. She must have been reprimanded, threatened even.

'I wanted to ask you for a simple piece of information. Have you ever worked at the prosecutor's house?'

'I worked there two years ago!'

'That's what I thought! As a cook? As a maid?'

'No, he doesn't have maid, he has a manservant!'

'Of course! . . . In that case, you did the heavy house-work . . . It must have been you who waxed the floors, dusted—'

'I was the cleaner!'

'Exactly! And so you must have discovered some of his little secrets! How long ago was that?'

'I left a year ago!'

'In other words, you were as beautiful a girl as you are today . . . of course!'

Maigret wasn't laughing. He had a particular gift for

saying things in an admirably convincing tone. Besides, Rosalie wasn't ugly. She had lavish curves that must have attracted plenty of wandering hands.

'Did the prosecutor come and watch you work?'

'That would have been the last straw! As if I'd have allowed him to hang around while I was scrubbing the floors!'

One thing made Rosalie soften, and that was seeing Madame Maigret doing little household chores. She watched her rather than Maigret, and at one point she couldn't help saying, 'I'll bring you a little brush . . . We've got some downstairs . . . it's too tiring with the broom.'

'Did the prosecutor entertain a lot of women?'

'I don't know!'

'Yes you do! Answer me nicely, Rosalie! You're not only a beautiful girl, you are also a good girl, and you'll remember that I was the only person to take your side, the other day, when they were insinuating—'

'It still wouldn't be any use!'

'What?'

'For me to talk! First of all it would ruin Albert's chances – he's my fiancé – because he wants to get a job in the civil service . . . Then I'd be locked up! . . . They all think I'm mad because I have dreams at night and I tell people about them.'

She became animated. All Maigret needed to do was egg her on a little.

'You were talking of a scandal—'

'If only that was all!'

'So, you were telling me that Monsieur Duhourceau didn't have women visitors! But he often goes to Bordeaux—'

'I don't give a fig about that!'

'So what scandal?'

'Anyone can tell you about it . . . It was public knowledge . . . A good two years ago . . . a package arrived at the post office, a little recorded delivery package that came from Paris . . . And when the postman went to pick it up, he saw that the label had come off . . . No one knew who it was for . . . There was no sender's address.

'At the post office they waited a week before opening it, because they hoped someone would come and claim it. And guess what they found?

'Photographs! But not your usual photographs . . . Nothing but naked women . . . And not just women . . . Couples—

'So, for two or three days, everyone was wondering who in Bergerac received such things . . . The postmaster had even called the inspector—

'Well, one fine day, another package arrived, wrapped in the same distinctive paper . . . The package was addressed to Monsieur Duhourceau! There!'

Maigret was not at all surprised. Had he not come to the conclusion earlier – solitary vice?

It wasn't to count his money that the old man shut himself away in his dark first-floor study at night! It was to gaze at his photographs, and probably licentious books too.

'Listen to me, Rosalie! I promise I won't mention you!

Admit that when you found out what you have just told me, you went and looked in the bookcases—'

'Who told you? . . . In the first place, the lower ones had mesh over them and were always locked . . . Only once did I find one with its key in the lock.'

'And what did you see?'

'You know very well! I even had nightmares for days and I couldn't let Albert touch me for a month—'

Hmm! Her relationship with the fair-haired fiancé was becoming clearer!

'Very fat books, weren't they? On beautiful paper with engravings—'

'Yes . . . and others . . . Things that are unthinkable.'

Was that Monsieur Duhourceau's entire secret? If so, it was pathetic! A sad individual, a bachelor, isolated in Bergerac where he couldn't smile at a woman without causing a scandal—

He consoled himself by becoming a book lover in his own way, collecting saucy etchings, erotic photographs, albums and catalogues politely referred to as 'collectors' books'.

And he was afraid.

Except that his hobby hardly had any connection with the two murdered women, or, more to the point, with Samuel!

Unless it was Samuel who supplied his photos? Yes? No? . . . Maigret wasn't sure. Rosalie shifted her weight from one foot to the other, very red in the face, taken aback at having said so much.

'If your wife hadn't been here, I'd never have dared—'

'Did Doctor Rivaud often come to visit Monsieur Duhourceau?'

'Almost never! He used to telephone him!'

'No one from his family?'

'Except for Mademoiselle Françoise, who acted as his secretary!'

'The prosecutor's?'

'Yes! She even brought over a little typewriter which was kept in a case.'

'Did she deal with legal matters?'

'I don't know what she dealt with, but she worked in a separate little office that was divided off from the library by a curtain . . . A heavy green velvet curtain.'

'And—?' began Maigret.

'I didn't say that! I never saw anything!'

'It didn't last?'

'Six months . . . Then Mademoiselle Françoise went to her mother's in Paris, or Bordeaux, I'm not sure exactly—'

'In short, Monsieur Duhourceau never made a pass at you?'

'I'd have given him what for!'

'And you know nothing! Thank you! I promise you no one will bother you, and your fiancé won't know that you came here this evening.'

After she had left, Madame Maigret closed the door and sighed, 'It makes you sick! . . . Intelligent men, in responsible positions—'

Madame Maigret was always incredulous when she learned something ugly. She could not even conceive of the possibility of instincts more perverted than her own, those of a decent wife, sad not to have children.

'Do you not think that the girl might have been exaggerating? If you want my opinion, she's trying to draw attention to herself! She'll say anything, as long as someone will listen to her! And I'll bet she was never attacked.'

'So do I!'

'The same with the doctor's sister-in-law. She's not very strong. You could knock her down with a feather. And she supposedly managed to fight the man off?'

'You're right!'

'I'll go even further! I think that if this goes on, within a week no one will be able to distinguish between the truth and lies! These stories are firing people's imaginations! In the morning, they tell stories they have imagined at night as they fall asleep, as if they had actually happened. Already Monsieur Duhourceau is becoming a dirty old man! Tomorrow, they'll be saying that the police inspector is unfaithful to his wife and that . . . but you! What on earth could they be saying about you? . . . For there's no reason why they shouldn't be talking about you. One of these days I'll have to show them our marriage certificate if I don't want them to think I'm your mistress.'

Maigret looked at her, laughing affectionately. She was getting carried away. All these complications terrified her.

'It's like this doctor who isn't a doctor—'

'Says who?'

'What do you mean, says who? Seeing as I telephoned all the universities, all the medical schools, and—'

'Give me my herb tea, would you?'

'That at least won't do you any harm, because it wasn't prescribed by him.'

As he drank, he held his wife's hand in his. It was warm in the room. A wisp of steam rose from the radiator with a regular hissing sound, like the purring of a tomcat.

Downstairs, dinner was over. The games of backgammon and billiards were beginning.

'A nice cup of herb tea, it's just what—'

'Yes, darling, a nice cup of herb tea—'

And he kissed her hand with a tenderness disguised by irony.

'You'll see! If all goes well, in two or three days, we'll be back home.'

'And you'll start on a new case!'

9. The Kidnapping of the Cabaret Singer

Maigret was amused at Leduc's discomfiture as he grumbled, 'What do you mean, entrust me with a sensitive mission?'

'A mission that only you are capable of carrying out! Come, don't give me that look! It's not a matter of burgling the prosecutor's house or of breaking and entering the Rivauds' villa.'

And Maigret drew a Bordeaux newspaper towards him, underscoring a classified advertisement with his fingernail.

Solicitor is seeking a Madame Beausoleil, formerly of Algiers, concerning an inheritance. Contact Maigret, Hôtel d'Angleterre, Bergerac. Urgent.

Leduc did not laugh. He looked at his colleague with annoyance.

'You want me to play the lawyer?'

And he said this so grudgingly that Madame Maigret, who was on the other side of the room, couldn't help laughing.

'Of course not! The advert appeared in ten local papers in the Bordeaux region and in the main Paris dailies.'

'Why Bordeaux?'

'Don't worry. How many trains a day stop in Bergerac?'

'Three or four!'

'The weather's neither too hot nor too cold. It's not raining. Is there a café by the station? Yes. So this is your mission: be on the platform when each train arrives until you spot Madame Beausoleil.'

'But I don't know her!'

'Neither do I! I don't even know whether she's fat or thin. She must be between forty and sixty. And I have a feeling that she's probably fat.'

'But given that the ad says to come here, I don't see why I—'

'Very smart! The thing is, I suspect that there'll be a third person at the station, who will try and stop the lady from coming here. Mission understood? Bring the lady here. Without fail!'

Maigret had never seen Bergerac station but he had in front of him a postcard with a picture of it. It showed the platform bathed in sunlight, the stationmaster's little office, the lamp room.

It was quite a delight to imagine poor old Leduc, with his straw hat, pacing up and down while waiting for each train, scrutinizing the passengers, following all the mature ladies and asking them if they were Madame Beausoleil.

'Can I count on you?'

'Since it has to be done!'

And he left, cutting a sorry figure. They saw him trying to start his car, and, failing to do so, turning the starting handle for ages.

A little later, Doctor Rivaud's assistant, who was now

looking after Maigret, came into the room, greeting Madame Maigret and then the inspector profusely.

He was a shy, bony, ginger-haired young man who kept banging into the furniture, apologizing with a string of 'I'm sorry's.

'Excuse me, madame . . . Can you tell me where I can find some hot water?'

And, as he nearly knocked over the bedside table, 'I'm sorry! Oh! I'm sorry.'

As he tended Maigret, he was anxious, 'I'm not hurting you? I'm sorry. Could you possibly sit up a little straighter? I'm sorr—'

Maigret smiled as he thought of Leduc parking his old Ford in front of the station.

'Has Doctor Rivaud got a lot of work?'

'Yes, he's very busy. He's always very busy.'

'He's a fairly active man, isn't he?'

'Very active! I mean he's extraordinary! . . . I'm sorry! . . . When you think he starts work at seven in the morning, with the free consultations . . . Then he has his surgery . . . Then the hospital . . . Mind you, he doesn't rely on his juniors, like so many others, he insists on seeing each patient himself.'

'Has it ever occurred to you that he might not be a doctor?'

The young man nearly choked, and decided to laugh.

'You're joking! Doctor Rivaud isn't a doctor, he's a very great doctor. And, if he wanted to live in Paris, he would soon have a unique reputation.'

His opinion was sincere. Maigret could sense the young man's genuine admiration, devoid of any ulterior motive.

'Do you know which medical school he trained at?'

'Montpellier, I think. Yes! That's it . . . He told me about his teachers there. Then he was a junior doctor, in Paris, under Doctor Martel.'

'Are you certain?'

'In his laboratory, I saw a photograph of Doctor Martel surrounded by all his students.'

'That's odd.'

'I'm sorry! Did it really occur to you that Doctor Rivaud might not be a real doctor?'

'Not especially . . .'

'I'll say it again, and you can believe me, he's a genius! The only criticism I'd make is that he works too hard because at this rate, he'll soon be exhausted. Several times I've seen him in a frazzled state which—'

'Recently?'

'And at other times, yes! You've seen how he only allowed me to take over your care when he was certain you were on the mend. And yours isn't a particularly serious case. Anyone else would have handed over to his assistant from the first day.'

'Are his colleagues very fond of him?'

'They all admire him!'

'I'm asking you if they like him.'

'Yes . . . I think so . . . there's no reason—'

But there was a hint of reservation in his voice. The junior doctor clearly saw a distinction between admiration and affection.

'Do you often go to his house?'

'Never! I see him at the hospital every day.'

'So you don't know his family.'

Throughout this entire conversation, it was the usual routine, the familiar gestures that Maigret could now anticipate. The blind was down, muting the sunlight, but they could hear the sounds of the square.

'He has a pretty sister-in-law.'

The young man did not reply, pretending not to have heard.

'He often goes to Bordeaux, doesn't he?'

'He's called there sometimes! If he wanted to, he could be doing operations all over the place, Paris, Nice, and even overseas.'

'Despite his young age!'

'For a surgeon, that's an advantage! In general, older surgeons are not much sought after.'

They were done. The doctor washed his hands, looked for a towel, stammered at Madame Maigret who brought him one, 'Oh! Sorry . . .'

Some new features for Maigret to add to the portrait of Doctor Rivaud. His colleagues spoke of him as a genius, and he was frenetically busy!

Ambitious? Probably! And yet he didn't move to Paris, where it would have been natural for him to pursue his career.

'Do you make anything of all that?' said Madame Maigret when they were alone.

'Me? . . . Raise the blind, will you? . . . It's clear that Rivaud is a doctor. Otherwise he wouldn't be able to dupe his entourage for so long, especially at work, not in the privacy of his surgery, but in a hospital.'

'And yet, the universities . . .'

'One thing at a time. For now, I'm waiting for Leduc, who'll be very ill at ease with his companion. Did you not hear a train? If it's the one from Bordeaux, there's a chance that—'

'What are you hoping for?'

'You'll see! Pass me the matches.'

He was better. His temperature had dropped to 37.5 and the stiffness in his injured shoulder had almost gone. An even better sign was that he could no longer lie still in bed. He kept changing position, rearranging the pillows, sitting up and then stretching out.

'You must make a few phone calls,' he said to his wife.

'To whom?'

'I'd like to know the whereabouts of each person I'm interested in. Ask for the prosecutor, first of all. When you hear his voice on the other end, hang up.'

Madame Maigret did as instructed. Meanwhile, Maigret watched the square and puffed away at his pipe.

'He's at home!'

'Now, telephone the hospital. Ask for the doctor.'

He too was there!

'Now call his home. If it's his wife who answers, ask to speak to Françoise. And if it's Françoise, ask for Madame Rivaud.'

Madame Rivaud answered. She said her sister was out and asked if she could take a message.

'Hang up!'

All the people she called must have been intrigued and would spend the morning trying to identify the mystery caller!

Five minutes later, the hotel bus arrived from the station with three guests, and the boy took up their luggage. Then came the postman on his bicycle, bringing the postbag, which he dropped off at the post office.

Finally, the unmistakeable honking of the old Ford's horn, then the old Ford itself. As it pulled up in front of the hotel, Maigret saw that there was someone next to Leduc and he thought he spotted a third person on the rear seat.

He was not mistaken. Poor Leduc alighted first, looked about him anxiously, like a man who is afraid of being laughed at, then opened the door to a fat lady who nearly fell into his arms.

A young woman had already jumped out. The first thing she did was dart a furious look up at Maigret's window.

It was Françoise, dressed in a fetching pale green suit.

'May I stay?' asked Madame Maigret.

'Why not? . . . Open the door . . . They're on their way up.'

There was a racket on the stairs. They could hear the fat lady's laboured breathing. She came in mopping her brow.

'So the lawyer who isn't a lawyer is here!'

A common voice. And not just her voice! She could have been no older than forty-five. In any case, she still had pretentions to beauty, for she was made-up like a theatre girl.

A blonde with ample, flowing flesh and slightly petulant lips.

Looking at her, Maigret had the feeling he had seen her somewhere before. And suddenly he realized why – she was the stereotype, now rare, of the singer of bygone cabarets! Simpering. A tight-waisted dress. Provocative eyes. And milky, almost bare shoulders. That particular way of waddling and of looking at people the way a singer on stage looks at her audience.

'Madame Beausoleil?' asked Maigret gallantly. 'Do sit down . . . You too, mademoiselle.'

But Françoise did not sit down. She was very jumpy.

'I'm warning you,' she said. 'I'm going to make a formal complaint! We've never seen anything like it.'

Leduc stood by the door looking so sorry for himself that it was clear things had not been straightforward.

'Calm down, mademoiselle. And forgive me for having wanted to see your mother.'

'Who says she's my mother?'

Madame Beausoleil was confused. She looked from Maigret, who was very calm, to Françoise bristling with anger.

'At least I presume she is, since you went to meet her at the station.'

'Mademoiselle wanted to stop her mother from coming here!' sighed Leduc, who was staring at the rug.

'So what did you do?'

It was Françoise who replied, 'He threatened us. He spoke of an arrest warrant, as if we were thieves. Let him show us this arrest warrant, otherwise—'

And she reached towards the telephone. It was obvious

that Leduc had somewhat overstepped his role. He wasn't proud of himself.

'I could see they were about to make a scene in the waiting room!'

'Just a moment, mademoiselle. Who do you want to call?'

'But . . . the prosecutor—'

'Sit down! Mind you, I'm not preventing you from calling him. On the contrary! But perhaps, for everyone's sake, it would be better not to be in too much of a hurry.'

'Mother, I forbid you to reply!'

'Me? I haven't a clue what's going on! Now, are you a lawyer or a police inspector?'

'Detective Chief Inspector!'

And she gestured as if to say, 'In that case—'

You could sense she was a woman who had already had dealings with the police and who respected or at least feared that institution.

'I still don't see why, I—'

'Don't worry, madame . . . Everything will soon become clear . . . I simply want to ask you a few questions and—'

'There's no inheritance?'

'I don't know yet.'

'That's horrible!' muttered Françoise. 'Mother, don't answer!'

She couldn't keep still. She was tearing her handkerchief to shreds, and sometimes she glared at Leduc with loathing.

'I presume that your profession is that of opera singer?'

He knew that those two little words would tickle her vanity.

'Yes, monsieur . . . I sang at the Olympia in the days when—'

'Indeed, I do believe I remember your name . . . Beausoleil . . . Yvonne, isn't it?'

'Joséphine Beausoleil! . . . But the doctors advised me to go somewhere warm, and I went on tours to Italy, Turkey, Syria, Egypt—'

In the days of the cabarets! He could easily picture her, on the stage of the famous establishments that were all the rage in Paris, frequented by all the city's dandies and officers. Then she would come down among the audience, going from table to table with a tray in her hand, and drink champagne with the customers.

'Did you end up in Algeria?'

'Yes! But I had my first daughter in Cairo.'

Françoise was on the verge of throwing a tantrum. Or rushing at Maigret!

'Father unknown?'

'Excuse me, I knew him very well! An English officer serving with—'

'And you had your second daughter, Françoise, in Algeria—'

'Yes . . . and that was the end of my theatrical career. Actually, I was ill for quite a long time. By the time I recovered, I had lost my voice—'

'And?'

'Françoise's father looked after me, until he was called back to France. He was a customs official, you see—'

This confirmed everything that Maigret had suspected. Now, he could piece together the life of the mother and the two daughters in Algiers. The still-attractive Joséphine Beausoleil had earnest suitors. The girls were growing up. Wouldn't they naturally follow in their mother's footsteps?

The eldest was sixteen . . .

'I wanted them to be dancers! Because dancing is less thankless than singing! Especially abroad! Germaine started having lessons with an old friend who was living in Algiers—'

'And she fell ill—'

'Did she tell you? . . . That's right, she'd never been very strong . . . Perhaps from having moved around so much when she was little! . . . Because I didn't want to leave her with a nanny . . . I used to sling a sort of cradle between the luggage racks in the train compartment.'

A decent woman, in other words. She was very relaxed now. She didn't even appear to understand why her daughter was so furious. Wasn't Maigret speaking to her politely, with consideration? And he used simple words that she could understand.

She was an artiste. She had travelled. She'd had lovers, then children. Wasn't that in the nature of things?

'Did she have chest problems?'

'No! It was her head. She was always complaining of headaches. Then, one fine day, she caught meningitis and had to be rushed to hospital—'

A pause. Up till now, she had been happy to talk openly. But Joséphine Beausoleil had reached the critical point.

She no longer knew what she ought to say and her eyes sought out Françoise.

'The inspector hasn't got the right to question you, Mother. Don't tell him any more.'

Easier said than done. Madame Beausoleil knew that it wasn't a good idea to get on the wrong side of the police. She would have liked to please everyone.

Leduc had perked up again and was signalling to Maigret with a look that said, 'We're getting somewhere.'

'Look, madame . . . you can choose whether to talk or remain silent, that is your right. However, you might find yourself being forced to speak in different surroundings, in court for example.'

'But I haven't done anything wrong!'

'Exactly! That's why, in my view, it's wiser to talk. As for you, Mademoiselle Françoise—'

She wasn't listening. She had picked up the telephone and was speaking in an anxious tone, covertly glancing at Leduc as if afraid he would snatch the receiver from her hands.

'Hello! . . . He's at the hospital? . . . It doesn't matter! . . . Call him now . . . Or rather tell him to come to the Hôtel d'Angleterre without a moment's delay . . . Yes! . . . He'll understand . . . Tell him Françoise called!'

She listened for a moment longer, hung up and looked at Maigret coldly, defiantly.

'He'll come. Don't talk, Mother.'

She was shaking. Beads of perspiration ran down her forehead, plastering her chestnut hair to her temples.

'You see, inspector—'

'Mademoiselle Françoise . . . you'll note that I did not prevent you from telephoning . . . Quite the opposite! . . . I've stopped questioning your mother . . . Now, do you want a piece of advice? . . . Telephone Monsieur Duhourceau too. He is at home.'

Françoise tried to fathom out what he was up to. She hesitated but eventually she apprehensively picked up the phone.

'Hello! . . . One-six-seven, please.'

'Come over here, Leduc.'

And Maigret whispered something in his ear. Leduc looked surprised, embarrassed.

'Do you think that—?'

He left the room abruptly and soon they could see him turning the starting handle on his car.

'This is Françoise . . . Yes . . . I'm telephoning from the inspector's room . . . my mother is here . . . Yes! The inspector is requesting that you come . . . No! . . . No! . . . No, I swear—'

And this torrent of *nos* was uttered with vehemence, with fear.

No, I tell you!

She remained standing by the table, ramrod straight.

Maigret, lighting his pipe, watched her with a smile, while Joséphine Beausoleil powdered her nose.

10. *The Note*

The silence had lasted for a few minutes when Maigret saw Françoise flinch as she stared out at the square, then abruptly turn away looking anxious.

Madame Rivaud was crossing the square, making for the hotel. Optical illusion? Or was it the fact that something serious was happening that gave everything a sinister air? Whatever it was, seen from a distance, she looked like a character from a play. She seemed to be propelled forwards by an invisible force which she did not attempt to resist.

Soon they could make out her face. It was pale. Her hair was a mess. Her coat was not done up.

'Here's Germaine—' said Madame Beausoleil at last. 'Someone must have told her I was here.'

Madame Maigret automatically went to open the door. And when they saw Madame Rivaud close up, it was clear that something terrible was happening to her.

She forced herself to remain calm and smiling. But there was something distracted in her gaze. She couldn't prevent her features from suddenly crumpling.

'Excuse me, inspector . . . I heard that my mother and sister were here and—'

'Who told you?'

'Who?' she echoed, trembling.

What a difference between her and Françoise! Madame Rivaud was the unlucky one, the woman who had retained her coarse looks and was probably treated without the slightest respect. Even her mother looked at her with a certain severity.

'What do you mean, you don't know who?'

'It was on the road—'

'You haven't seen your husband?'

'Oh no! . . . No! . . . I swear I haven't.'

And Maigret, concerned, looked from one woman to the other and then towards the main square. Leduc had not arrived yet. What could that mean? The inspector had wanted to ensure that the surgeon would remain at his disposal. He had tasked Leduc with watching him and, preferably, with bringing him to the hotel.

He was not paying any attention to Madame Maigret. He looked from Madame Rivaud's dusty shoes – she must have run along the road – to Françoise's drawn face.

Suddenly Madame Maigret leaned over him and murmured, 'Give me your pipe.'

He was about to protest. But he noticed that she had dropped a scrap of paper on to the bed. And he read:

Madame Rivaud has just slipped a note to her sister, who is holding it in her palm.

There was bright sunshine outside. All the sounds of the town whose music and rhythms Maigret knew by heart. Madame Beausoleil sat upright in her chair, waiting, like a woman who knew how to conduct herself. Madame

Rivaud, on the other hand, was incapable of composing herself, bringing to mind a naughty schoolgirl who has just been caught out.

'Mademoiselle Françoise—' began Maigret.

She was trembling from head to foot. For a second, her gaze met Maigret's. It was the sharp, steely gaze of a person who does not lose their head.

'Would you come over here for a moment and—'

Dear Madame Maigret! Had she guessed what was about to happen? She whirled round and rushed to the door. But Françoise had already made a dash for it. She raced along the corridor and was already on the stairs.

'What is she doing?' asked Joséphine Beausoleil in alarm.

Maigret did not move, could not move. Nor could he send his wife after the fugitive.

'When did your husband give you the note?' he merely asked Madame Rivaud.

'What note?'

What was the point of starting a painful interrogation? Maigret called his wife.

'Go to a window that looks out on the rear of the hotel.'

This was the moment the prosecutor chose to make his entrance. He was starchy and formal. He wore a severe, almost threatening expression, probably because he was afraid.

'I received a phone call telling me—'

'Sit down, Monsieur Duhourceau.'

'But . . . the person who telephoned me . . .'

'Françoise has just run away. It is possible that she will

be caught, but it is equally possible that she won't! Please, sit down. You know Madame Beausoleil, I believe?'

'Me? Not at all!'

And he tried to follow Maigret's gaze. For it was clear that the inspector was talking for the sake of it, while his mind was elsewhere, or rather while giving the impression he was watching a performance that was for his eyes only. He was watching the square, listening out for something and staring at Madame Rivaud.

Suddenly there was a violent commotion inside the hotel. People began running down the stairs. Doors banged. It even sounded as though a shot had been fired.

'What . . . what—?'

Shouts. Crockery smashing. Then sounds of a chase again, on the floor above, and a window shattering, the fragments falling on to the pavement.

Madame Maigret rushed back into the room, locking the door behind her.

'I think Leduc has—' she gasped.

'Leduc?' echoed the prosecutor suspiciously.

'Doctor Rivaud's car was in the little street behind the hotel. The doctor was there, waiting for someone. Just as Françoise reached the door and was about to get into the car, Leduc's old Ford arrived. I nearly shouted to him to hurry. I saw him sitting at the wheel . . . But he had his own ideas and he calmly shot at one of the doctor's tyres and punctured it.

'The pair didn't know where to go. The doctor spun around like a weather vane . . . When he saw Leduc getting out of his car, his gun still in his hand, he pushed the girl into the hotel and they both ran—

'Leduc chased them along the corridors . . . They're up there—'

'I still don't understand!' said the prosecutor, ashen-faced.

'What happened earlier? It's easy! I placed a classified advertisement which brought Madame Beausoleil here. The doctor did not want this meeting to take place, so he sent Françoise to the station to stop her mother from coming.

'I had foreseen that. I had Leduc watching the arrivals and instead of bringing me one, he brought both of them.

'You'll see, everything will fall into place. Françoise, sensing that their whole life is going to be ruined, tele-phones her brother-in-law to ask him to come.

'Meanwhile, I send Leduc to watch Rivaud . . . Leduc reaches the hospital too late . . . The doctor has already left . . . He's at home . . . He writes a note for Françoise and gets his wife to come here and slip it to her discreetly.

'Do you follow? . . . He sits in his car in the little street behind the hotel . . . He's waiting for Françoise so they can run off together.

'Half a minute more and they'd have got away . . . Except that Leduc arrived in his Ford, suspected that some-thing fishy was going on, punctured one of Rivaud's tyres and—'

As he spoke, the racket in the hotel grew louder in the space of a few seconds. It was coming from upstairs. But what was going on?

And then, suddenly, a deathly hush! Awed by the silence, everyone froze.

Leduc's voice was barking orders, on the floor above. But they didn't understand what he was saying.

A dull thud . . . A second . . . A third . . . Finally, the crash of a door being kicked in.

They were expecting more sounds and the wait was excruciating. Why was no one moving about overhead any more? Why the slow, calm tread of just one man?

Madame Rivaud opened her eyes wide. The prosecutor tugged at his moustache. Joséphine Beausoleil was on the verge of bursting into nervous tears.

'They must be dead!' said Maigret slowly, gazing up at the ceiling.

'What? . . . What are you saying?'

Madame Rivaud became animated, rushing over to the inspector, distraught, her eyes wild.

'It's not true! Say it's not true!'

More steps . . . The door opened . . . Leduc came in, a stray lock of hair on his forehead, his jacket half torn off, looking grief-stricken.

'Dead?'

'Both of them!'

With outstretched arms he stopped Madame Rivaud who wanted to leave the room.

'Not now.'

'It's not true! I know it's not true! I want to see him.'

She was breathless. Meanwhile, her mother did not know what attitude to take.

And Monsieur Duhourceau stared at the rug. Anyone

would think that he was the most dismayed, the most shattered by this news.

'How come, both of them?' he eventually stammered, turning to Leduc.

'I was chasing them up the stairs and along the corridors. They managed to get into a room and lock it before I reached them . . . I'm not strong enough to kick in such a heavy door. I sent for the owner, who's brawny . . . I could see them through the keyhole.'

Germaine Rivaud glared at him like a madwoman. Leduc looked at Maigret, seeking approval to continue speaking.

Why not? They had to see this tragedy through to the end and get to the truth.

'They were embracing . . . She was especially anxious as he held her in his arms . . . She was saying, *"I don't want to . . . Not that! . . . No! . . . Rather—"*

'And it was she who took his gun out of his pocket. She put it in his hand. I heard, *"Shoot . . . Shoot while you're kissing me."*

'I didn't see anything because the owner arrived and—'

He mopped his forehead. His knees were visibly trembling beneath his trousers.

'We were no more than twenty seconds too late, Rivaud was already dead when I leaned over him . . . Françoise had her eyes open . . . At first I thought it was all over . . . But just when I least expected it—'

'Well?' The prosecutor almost sobbed.

'She smiled at me . . . I've had a sign put up barring access to the corridor . . . Nobody is to touch anything . . . We called the hospital—'

Joséphine Beausoleil did not appear to have grasped what Leduc had told them. She stared at him, dazed. Then she turned to Maigret and said in a dreamy voice, 'It can't be true, can it?'

Suddenly the room erupted into action around Maigret, who remained immobile in bed. The door opened and the hotel owner's flushed face appeared. His breath reeked of alcohol as he spoke.

He must have emptied a large glass at the bar to steady his nerves. The shoulder of his white jacket was torn and dirty.

'It's the doctor . . . Shall—?'

'I'll go!' said Leduc, reluctantly.

'You're here, Monsieur Duhourceau? . . . You know? . . . If you could see it! . . . It's enough to make you cry your eyes dry . . . And they're beautiful, the pair of them! . . . They look like—'

'Leave us!' shouted Maigret.

'Should I lock the main door? . . . People are beginning to gather in the square . . . The inspector isn't at the police station . . . Some officers are on their way, but—'

When Maigret sought Germaine Rivaud's eyes, he found her stretched out on Madame Maigret's bed, her head on the pillow. She wasn't crying or sobbing, but lay emitting long, woeful groans like a wounded animal.

As for Madame Beausoleil, she wiped her eyes, rose and asked spiritedly, 'Can I go up and see them?'

'Later . . . When the doctor's finished—'

Madame Maigret hovered over Germaine Rivaud, unable to find any way of comforting her. And the prosecutor sighed, 'I told you—'

The noises from the street rose up to the room. Two officers arrived on bicycles, forcing their way through the crowd. Some onlookers protested.

Maigret filled a pipe, gazing out, looking straight – without realizing it – at the little grocer's store opposite, whose customers he now knew by heart.

'Did you leave the child in Bordeaux, Madame Beausoleil?'

She turned to the prosecutor for guidance.

'I . . . yes—'

'The child must be three by now?'

'Two.'

'Is it a boy?'

'A little girl . . . But—'

'Françoise's daughter, is that right?'

And the prosecutor, rising with a determined air, 'Detective Chief Inspector, I ask you to—'

'You're right . . . Later . . . Or rather, on my first outing, I'll take the liberty of paying you a visit.'

He had the impression that the prosecutor was relieved.

'By then, it will all be over . . . What am I saying? It is all over now, isn't it? . . . Don't you think you should be upstairs, where the public prosecutor's presence is required?'

In his haste, the prosecutor forgot to take his leave. He fled like a schoolboy suddenly released from detention.

And, once the door had closed behind him, a different kind of intimacy developed. Germaine was still groaning. She remained deaf to Madame Maigret's entreaties as she placed cold-water compresses on her forehead. But the patient brushed them off impatiently and the water was gradually soaking into the pillow.

Joséphine Beausoleil sat down again beside Maigret, with a sigh.

'Who could have imagined such a thing!'

A good woman at heart! Fundamentally moral! She thought of her life as normal, ordinary! Could anyone hold it against her?

Her creased eyelids began to swell and soon tears were running down her cheeks, diluting their blush.

'She was your favourite—'

She showed no concern for Germaine, who was probably not listening anyway.

'Of course! She was beautiful, so delicate! And so much cleverer than her sister! It's not Germaine's fault! She was always ill. It hindered her development. When the doctor wanted to marry Germaine, Françoise was too young. Barely thirteen . . . Well, believe it or not, I thought there'd be trouble sooner or later . . . and I was right.'

'What was Rivaud called, in Algiers?'

'Doctor Meyer . . . I suppose there's no point lying any more . . . Besides, if you did all this, it's because you already knew.'

'Was it he who helped his father run away from the hospital? . . . Samuel Meyer?'

'Yes . . . And that's even how it all started with Germaine . . . There were only three patients in the meningitis ward . . . my daughter, Samuel, as he was called, and another . . . So one night, the doctor set the place on fire . . . He had always sworn that the other patient, the one who burned to death in the fire and who afterwards passed for Meyer, was already dead . . . I'm inclined to believe it, because he wasn't a bad boy . . . He could have chosen to abandon his father, who had done some stupid things.'

'I understand! So the other man's death was registered as that of Samuel Meyer . . . The doctor married Germaine . . . He brought the three of you to France—'

'Not right away . . . First he went to Spain . . . He was waiting for some documents that didn't come.'

'Samuel?'

'He had been sent to America and warned never to set foot in Europe again. He already seemed like a man who wasn't in his right mind.'

'Finally, your son-in-law received documents in the name of Rivaud. He came and settled here with his wife and sister-in-law. What about you?'

'He gave me a little allowance to stay in Bordeaux . . . I would have preferred Marseille, for instance, or Nice . . . Especially Nice! But he wanted to keep me close by . . . He worked very hard . . . Despite what people may say about him, he was a good doctor who would never have harmed a patient for—'

Maigret had closed the window to keep out the noise from the street. The radiators were pumping out heat. The smell of pipe smoke filled the room.

Germaine was still groaning like a child, and her mother explained, 'Since she underwent trepanation, it's been even worse than before. She wasn't very cheerful in the first place . . . To think! A child who spent her youth in bed! . . .

Afterwards, the slightest thing would make her cry. And she was afraid of everything.'

Bergerac had not guessed a thing! Her entire troubled, tragic life had been grafted on to her provincial town life, and no one had the least idea.

People said, *the doctor's villa . . . the doctor's car . . . the doctor's wife . . . the doctor's sister-in-law.*

And they saw only the neat, pretty villa, the expensive car with its streamlined bonnet, the sporty young woman with nervous mannerisms, the slightly downtrodden wife.

In some bourgeois apartment in Bordeaux, Madame Beausoleil was enjoying a comfortable retirement after a turbulent life. She who'd had so many worries about the future, who'd depended on the whims of so many men, could at last live the life of a woman of private means!

She must have earned the respect of her neighbours. She had her habits. She paid her suppliers on time.

And when her daughters came to see her, it was in a swanky car.

Now she was crying again. She blew her nose in a hand-kerchief that was too small, and almost entirely made of lace.

'If only you had known Françoise . . . Listen! . . . When she came to give birth at my place . . . Because that's where it happened . . . We can talk in front of Germaine! . . . She knows all about—'

Madame Maigret listened, appalled. She was discovering a terrifying world.

Cars were parked beneath the window. The forensic

pathologist had arrived, and so had the investigating magistrate, the clerk and the inspector, who had finally been found at a neighbouring village fair where he had gone to buy rabbits.

There was a knock at the door. It was Leduc, who looked at Maigret shyly to find out if he could come in.

'Leave us, would you?'

It was better to remain in this intimate atmosphere. But all the same, Leduc came over to the bed and whispered, 'If they still want to see them where they fell—'

'No! No!'

What was the use? Madame Beausoleil was waiting for the intruder to leave. She was in a hurry to go on with telling her secrets. This big man lying in bed, who looked at her benevolently, made her feel safe.

He understood her. He didn't show surprise. He didn't ask stupid questions.

'I think you were talking about Françoise—'

'Yes . . . Well, when the baby was born . . . But . . . You probably don't know the whole story yet—'

'I do!'

'Did she tell you?'

'Monsieur Duhourceau was there!'

'Yes! I've never seen a man so distraught, so unhappy . . . He kept saying it was a crime to bring babies into the world because there was always the risk the mother would die . . . He listened to the screams . . . I tried giving him a few little drinks—'

'Is your apartment big?'

'Two bedrooms.'

'Was there a midwife?'

'Yes . . . Rivaud didn't want to take the responsibility on his own . . . So—'

'Do you live near the port?'

'Just by the bridge, in a little street where—'

Another scene that Maigret could visualize as clearly as if he had been present. But at the same time, he saw another – the one taking place at that moment, above his head.

Rivaud and Françoise, whom the doctor, helped by the undertakers, was forcibly separating.

The prosecutor, who must have been whiter than the paper of the forms that the clerk was filling in with a shaking hand.

And the police inspector, who, an hour earlier at the market, had only been concerned with his rabbits!

'When Monsieur Duhourceau heard it was a girl, he began to cry and, as true as I sit before you, he laid his head on my breast . . . I even thought he was going to pass out . . . I tried to stop him from going in, because—'

And she paused again, distrustful, looking at Maigret covertly.

'I'm just a poor woman who's always done her best . . . It wouldn't be nice to take advantage of—'

Germaine Rivaud had stopped groaning. Perched on the edge of the bed, she stared straight ahead of her looking lost.

It was the hardest moment. The bodies were being carried down on stretchers, which could be heard banging into the walls.

The heavy, cautious footfall of the bearers descending one stair at a time.

And a voice saying, 'Mind the banister!'

A little later, there was a knock on the door. It was Leduc again, reeking of alcohol like the hotel owner. 'It's over,' he stammered.

And so it was. Outside an engine started up.

11. *The Father*

'Say Detective Chief Inspector Maigret is here!'

He couldn't help smiling, because this was his first outing and he was happy to be walking around like everyone else! He was even proud, as proud as a child taking its first steps!

Even so, he had a weak, unsteady walk. Since the manservant had forgotten to invite him to sit down, he had to drag a chair towards him, for, worryingly, he could already feel beads of sweat gathering on his forehead.

The manservant, with a striped waistcoat! A peasant farmer type promoted to a higher rank, and who was inordinately proud of the fact!

'If monsieur would be so good as to follow me . . . Monsieur Duhourceau will see monsieur straight away.'

The manservant had no idea that a staircase could be an effort to climb. Maigret held on to the banister. He felt hot. He counted the stairs.

Another eight.

'This way . . . One moment—'

And the house was exactly as Maigret had imagined it! He was in the famous first-floor study that he had pictured so many times!

A white ceiling, with heavy varnished oak beams. A vast hearth. And above all, bookshelves lining the walls.

There was no one in the room. There was no sound of footsteps in the house, since all the floors were thickly carpeted.

So, despite his urgent need to sit down, Maigret walked over to the lower bookshelves where a metal grid and a green curtain hid the books from sight.

He had difficulty poking his finger through a hole in the lattice. He pulled back the curtain. Behind, there was nothing, only empty shelves!

And when he turned around, he saw the prosecutor, who had witnessed his action.

'I've been expecting you for two days . . . I confess—'

Maigret could have sworn he'd lost ten kilos! His cheeks were ravaged. And the lines around his mouth were twice as pronounced.

'Do sit down.'

Monsieur Duhourceau was ill at ease. He didn't dare look his visitor in the eye. He sat down in his usual place, at a desk laden with files.

Maigret judged it would be more charitable to get things over with in a few words. Several times the prosecutor had eluded him. Several times too he had taken his revenge. Now, he was coming close to regretting it.

A sixty-five-year-old man, all alone in that big house, all alone in the town where he was the most senior magistrate, all alone in his life.

'I see you have burned your books.'

There was no reply. Nothing but a faint blush on the old man's cheeks.

'Allow me first of all to get the judicial part of the

business out of the way. I think, at this point, everyone is agreed on that.

'Samuel Meyer, who is what I would call a bourgeois adventurer, in other words an out-and-out entrepreneur sailing in forbidden waters, has the ambition for his son to become someone important.

'Medical school . . . Doctor Meyer is taken on as Professor Martel's junior doctor. A brilliant future seems assured.

'Act One: Algiers. Old Meyer has a visit from a couple of his associates, who threaten him. He sends them to meet their maker.

'Act Two: Still in Algiers. He is sentenced to death. On the advice of his son, he feigns meningitis. And the son saves him.

'Is the man who will be buried in his stead already dead? That we will probably never know.

'Meyer junior, who now goes under the name of Rivaud, is not one of those men who need to pour out their feelings. He is strong and self-reliant.

'He's ambitious! A man of sharp intelligence, who knows his worth and wants to profit from it at all costs.

'Just one weakness: he falls vaguely in love with a young patient and he marries her, only to realize, after a while, that she holds no interest for him.'

The prosecutor did not move. For him too, this part of the story held no interest. He was far more apprehensive about what was to come.

'The new Rivaud sends his father to America. He settles down here with his wife and his young sister-in-law. And lastly he installs his mother-in-law in Bordeaux.

'And, of course, the inevitable happens. The girl living under his roof intrigues, annoys and eventually seduces him.

'Act Three: Right now, the public prosecutor is on the verge of discovering the truth about the Bergerac surgeon, through a channel that I do not yet know. Is that correct?'

And, clearly, without hesitation, Monsieur Duhourceau replied, 'That is correct.'

'So he has to be silenced. Rivaud knows that this prosecutor has a relatively inoffensive habit. Erotic books, euphemistically known as "collectors' books".

'It's a habit of elderly bachelors who have money and who find stamp-collecting too dull.

'Rivaud intends to make use of it . . . His sister-in-law is introduced to you as the perfect secretary. She'll come and help you with your filing . . . and she gradually forces you to woo her.

'Forgive me, Monsieur Duhourceau, it's not difficult. The hardest part is this: Françoise is pregnant . . . and it is crucial for Rivaud to have you at his mercy, that you should be convinced that the child is yours.'

'Rivaud does not want to have to run away again, change his name, look for a new job when he's beginning to build up a reputation for himself. The future is rosy.

'Françoise succeeds—

'And, of course, when she tells you she is going to be a mother, you fall for it.

'From now on, you will keep quiet! They've got you! Secret birth in Bordeaux, at Joséphine Beausoleil's, where you will continue to visit the child you believe is yours.

'It is Madame Beausoleil herself who told me.'

And Maigret, out of modesty, avoided looking at the prosecutor.

'Do you understand? Rivaud is a careerist! A superior man! A man who does not want to be hampered by his past! He truly loves his sister-in-law! Well! Despite that, his anxiety about the future is stronger and he tolerates the fact that she will lie in your arms at least once. It is the only question I will allow myself to ask you. Once?'

'Once!'

'Afterwards, she shied away, isn't that so?'

'She gave various excuses. She was ashamed—'

'No! She loved Rivaud! She only gave in to you to save him.'

Maigret still avoided looking over at the armchair where the prosecutor sat. He stared at the hearth where three big logs were burning.

'You are convinced that the baby is yours. Henceforth you will keep silent! You are invited to the villa. You go to Bordeaux to see your daughter.'

'And that's when things went seriously wrong. In America, Samuel – our Samuel from Poland and Algiers – has completely lost his mind. He attacked two women, in the suburbs of Chicago, and finished them off with a needle through the heart . . . I found that in the files . . .'

'A wanted man, he arrives in France . . . He has no more money . . . He reaches Bergerac . . . He's given money to disappear again, but, on leaving, he commits another crime in a fit of madness.

'The same! . . . Strangulation . . . Needle . . . In the

Moulin-Neuf woods, which run from the doctor's villa to the station . . . But you have already guessed the truth, haven't you?'

'No, I swear!'

'He comes back . . . He tries to kill again . . . He comes back again and he messes up . . . Each time, Rivaud gives him money to go away . . . He can't have him locked up . . . Even less can he have him arrested.'

'I told him it had to stop.'

'Yes! And he took the necessary steps. Old Samuel telephoned him. His son told him to jump off the train just before it reached the station.'

The prosecutor was pale, unable to utter a word, to make a movement.

'That's all! Rivaud killed him! He would not let anything come between him and the future for which he believed he was made. Not even his wife, whom he would have dispatched to a better world sooner or later! For he loved Françoise, with whom he had a daughter . . . The daughter who—'

'Enough!'

Then Maigret rose, simply, as if after any ordinary visit.

'It's over, Monsieur Duhourceau.'

'But—'

'They were a passionate couple, you see! A couple who would not let anything stand in their way! Rivaud had the wife he needed, Françoise, who for his sake allowed herself to lie in your arms—'

He was speaking only to a broken man incapable of responding.

'The two of them are dead . . . There remains a woman who has never been very bright, or very dangerous, Madame Rivaud, who will receive an allowance. She'll go and live with her mother in Bordeaux or elsewhere. Those two won't talk.'

He picked his hat up from a chair.

'As for me, it's time for me to get back to Paris, this is the end of my holiday.'

He took a few steps towards the desk and held out his hand.

'Goodbye, Monsieur Duhourceau.'

And, since the latter seized his hand with a gratitude that threatened to express itself in a torrent of words, he said in conclusion, 'No hard feelings!'

He followed the manservant in the striped waistcoat out, found the square basking in the sun, reached the Hôtel d'Angleterre without difficulty and said to the owner, 'For today, at last, poached truffles, foie gras . . . and the bill! . . . We're getting out of here!'

INSPECTOR MAIGRET

THE GRAND BANKS CAFÉ

GEORGES SIMENON

It was indeed a photo, a picture of a woman. But the face was completely hidden, scribbled all over in red ink. Someone had tried to obliterate the head, someone very angry. The pen had bitten into the paper. There were so many criss-crossed lines that not a single square millimetre had been left visible.

Captain Fallut's last voyage is shrouded in silence. To discover the truth about this doomed expedition, Maigret enters a remote, murky world of men on the margins of society; where fierce loyalties hide sordid affairs.

Translated by David Coward

Other Titles in the Series

A MAN'S HEAD
GEORGES SIMENON

He stared at Maigret, who stared back and found no trace of drunkenness in his companion's face.

Instead he saw the same eyes ablaze with acute intelligence which were now fixed on him with a look of consummate irony, as though Radek were truly possessed by fierce exultant joy.

An audacious plan to prove the innocence of a young drifter awaiting execution takes Maigret through the grey, autumnal streets of Paris. As he pursues the true culprit from lonely docks to elegant hotels and fashionable bars, he confronts the destructive power of a dangerously sharp intellect.

Translated by David Coward

OTHER TITLES IN THE SERIES

THE DANCER AT THE GAI-MOULIN
GEORGES SIMENON

They could not exactly hear the music. They could guess at it. What could be sensed above all was the beat from the drummer. A rhythm throbbing through the air and bringing back the image of the club's interior with its crimson velvet seats, the tinkle of glasses and the woman in pink dancing with a man in a tuxedo.

Maigret observes from a distance as two teenage boys are accused of killing a rich foreigner in a seedy club in Liège. As the disturbing truth about the man's death emerges, greed, pride and envy start to drive the two friends apart.

Translated by Siân Reynolds

INSPECTOR MAIGRET

OTHER TITLES IN THE SERIES

THE TWO-PENNY BAR
GEORGES SIMENON

A radiant late afternoon. The sunshine almost as thick as syrup in the quiet streets of the Left Bank . . . there are days like this, when ordinary life seems heightened, when the people walking down the street, the trams and cars all seem to exist in a fairy tale.

A story told by a condemned man leads Maigret to a bar by the Seine and into the sleazy underside of respectable Parisian life. In the oppressive heat of summer, a forgotten crime comes to life.

Translated by David Watson

Previously published as *The Bar on the Seine*

OTHER TITLES IN THE SERIES

And more to follow

www.penguin.com